QUEEN OF DIAMONDS
Text Copyright © 2018 Sandra Owens
Published by Sandra Owens
Print: ISBN-13: 978-0-9997864-2-0
e-Book: 978-0-9997864-3-7

Edits by: Melody Guy and Ella Sheridan
Printed in the United States of America

Cover Design and Interior Format

QUEEN OF
DIAMONDS

SANDRA
OWENS

DEDICATION

To all the Aces & Eights fans who patiently
(and not so patiently) waited for Kinsey's story.

ALSO BY SANDRA OWENS

~ Aces & Eights Series ~
Jack of Hearts
King of Clubs
Ace of Spades

~ K2 Team Series ~
Crazy for Her
Someone Like Her
Falling for Her
Lost in Her
Only Her

~ Regency Books ~
The Dukes Obsession
The Training of a Marquess
The Letter

℃

To sign up for Sandra's Newsletter go to:

https://bit.ly/2FVUPKS

CHAPTER ONE

KINSEY LANDON FINGERED THE MUCH read letter from her mother, and although she knew it by heart, she read it again.

My darling Kinsey,

If you are reading this, then I am no longer with you. Please don't cry too much, sweetheart. I've been blessed to have you in my life, and having you has kept me sane.

You see, I had three sons who were taken from me, and my heart has cried each day from missing them. Without you in my life, I don't know how I would have gone on.

I know I should have told you about your brothers, and I planned to, but I kept putting it off, unsure of how to explain walking away from my sons. You see, I left them for you.

The first time you asked about your father, I told you his name was John Landon and that he was dead. That was a lie, sweetheart. Maybe he's dead by now, I don't know, but your father's name was Gordon Gentry. He was not a nice man, Kinsey, but I would have stayed with him for my sons.

When he learned I was pregnant with you, he refused to believe he was your father. Of course he was! I don't know when he thought I'd had the time or opportunity to have an affair, as he controlled every minute of my life. He demanded I get rid of you, and when I refused, he tried to beat you out of my stomach. I knew then that to protect you, I had to leave.

It was the hardest decision of my life, leaving my boys with that man, but if I'd tried to take them, he would have hunted us down. My heart is still broken because I didn't have the courage or means to defy him.

But there was a life inside me. You. I had no choice but to protect you, my sweet girl. Fortunately, a man your father sometimes hired to do odd jobs took pity on me and helped me escape by driving me to the bus station. I will always owe him for that act of kindness because he helped me save you.

I had to believe that I had instilled in my sons honor and a love of learning so they would grow to be men I would be proud of. If you are asking where they are today, I don't know. All I can tell you is that their names are Alex, Court, and Nate Gentry, and that the last time I saw them, they were living in Ocala, Florida.

From the moment I knew you were in my belly, I have loved you, Kinsey. Please forgive me for not being honest with you before now.

You are a beautiful, intelligent woman, and I'm so very proud of you, daughter. If you should decide to find your brothers, please tell them why I left. Tell them that I never stopped loving them.

I only ask one thing of you, Kinsey. Be happy. I love you through eternity.

Mom.

Kinsey had found her mother's letter a year ago, only hours after Wanda Landon's funeral. Until that day Kinsey had thought she knew who she was. She'd believed she was the only beloved child of Wanda Landon, and that her father, John Landon, had died before she was a year old.

Now she knew the truth and the real reason she'd never been able to picture her father in her mind. It was impossible to have memories of a man who'd never existed. Yet she had imagined him, not so much his appearance but how he would have held her when she was a baby, how he would have looked down at his daughter with love in his eyes when she was cuddled in his arms. Sometimes she could almost remember him singing lullabies to her as she fell asleep.

Turned out that she only had those faint pictures in her mind because those were the things her mother had told her when she'd asked questions about him. She supposed that her mother had meant well when she created a fictional father for Kinsey, wanting her daughter to believe she had been loved and wanted by him. And wasn't that as far from the truth as possible?

All these years she'd mourned a father who never was, had always been sad that he hadn't lived to see his daughter grow up. She loved her mother dearly, missed her terribly, but she was having trouble forgiving her for the lies.

She folded the letter that had snatched the ground out from under her feet and put it back into the worn envelope. All her life, she'd thought she was Kinsey Landon, and that had been another lie. Should she change her last name?

"Kinsey Gentry," she said, testing the sound of it. Nope, it didn't feel like her. Although she didn't know who she was anymore. When her mother died, Kinsey had been left alone in the world, or so she'd thought until finding her mother's letter. After thinking long and hard, she'd made the decision to finish her last year of school before doing anything. Maybe it was her way of sticking her head in the sand, but she was still grieving her mother's death and was carrying a full class load while working part-time. There was no room on her schedule for looking for a family she hadn't known she had and wasn't sure she wanted.

But as soon as she'd graduated, her moratorium on doing nothing had ended. She was out of excuses, and it was either burn the letter and forget she'd ever read it, or find the Gentry brothers. It was still impossible to think of herself as their sister. All she wanted to do was see them, and then she could get on with her life.

After spending months searching for her brothers, she'd finally found their names on a business license for a biker bar in Miami called Aces & Eights, and that had ended her hope that they were men she'd want to know.

Still, she couldn't resist checking them out. They'd never know she was there. But she needed someone big and strong to go with her, and she knew just who to ask.

☾

"I need you to go with me to Aces and Eights. It's a biker bar."

"Huh?"

Kinsey lowered her menu, peering over the top at her friend. "I said, I need you to go—"

"I heard what you said." Aiden Calloway's eyebrows scrunched together. "I'm just trying to figure out why you said it."

"It's a long story." Aiden was one of her best friends. He'd been one of the University of Miami's star football players whose failing grades were going to get him kicked off the team in their freshman year if he didn't improve them. He'd hired her to tutor him, and they'd hit it off.

He was a good-looking guy, a ginger with gorgeous green eyes that women sighed over. Although not a top draft pick, he'd been signed by the Miami Dolphins, and she couldn't have been happier for him. He was also a big man, all muscle, and exactly what she needed for protection when she went to her brothers' bar. She couldn't imagine anyone daring to mess with him.

The waitress came to their table, and Kinsey ordered coffee, scrambled eggs, and wheat toast. Aiden went for the hungry man's breakfast with extra bacon.

"Jeez, Aiden, clogged arteries much?" she said after the waitress left.

"Growing boy here." He leaned back against the booth, spreading his arms along the top. "Okay, let's hear your long story."

"Read this," she said, handing Aiden her mother's letter.

As she watched his eyes scan the pages, she wondered why there had never been a sexual attraction between them. Oh, he had flirted outrageously when she'd first started tutoring him, but she'd quickly figured out that flirting was a part of his DNA. It hadn't taken long, though, for them to settle into a friendship, and he now saw her as an adopted sister that he had to watch over. Which was ridiculous, as she was perfectly capable of taking care of herself.

"Wow," he said, lifting his eyes to hers. "Are you going to try to find them?"

"I already have. They're owners of a biker bar here in Miami." At his raised eyebrows, she sighed. "Yeah, I know. Probably not the kind of men I want in my life, but I need to satisfy my curiosity."

"How long have you had this?" He waved the letter in front of her.

"A year." She reached over and snatched it away.

"And you're just now getting around to telling me?"

She'd known that was coming. It was the first time she'd shared the contents of the letter with anyone. The waitress delivered their breakfast, and she waited for the woman to leave before answering.

"I can't believe you're going to eat all that," she said, eyeing the pile of food in front of him.

He pointed his fork at her. "Stop evading my question. Why didn't you tell me?"

"Because I needed time to let it sink in and decide what I was going to do. But that's not the important thing. What are you doing Friday night?"

"Going to a biker bar?"

CHAPTER TWO

R AND STEVENS STOOD AT THE bar, contemplating his life and how he'd come to be the pretend owner of a biker bar. For a man who'd been born with a silver spoon in his mouth, who didn't drink, and who thought motorcycles were as dangerous as swimming in shark-infested waters, Aces & Eights was so far out of his element that it was laughable.

It was quiet, but it was still early. He glanced at his watch. Soon the bikers would start arriving, and a few hours after that the place would be packed, the music would be too loud, and the beer would be flowing.

The Gentry brothers actually owned Aces & Eights and had worked undercover from the bar for several years, but Nate Gentry was now special agent in charge of the Miami field office, Court Gentry was their new special agent in charge of intelligence, and their baby brother, Alex, was supervising undercover operations. Unlike Rand, the brothers had fit right in at Aces & Eights.

The low rumbles of motorcycles sounded. "And the games begin," he muttered.

"You say something, dude?"

Rand glanced at his partner, resisting the urge to roll his eyes. "Just thinking out loud. And I'm not your *dude*, dude." Josh Sheridan, his fellow FBI special agent, loved every minute of their undercover assignment. The kid was like a happy puppy nipping at his heels. Annoying but amusing.

Josh laughed. "Stop being so grumpy, old man."

Rand often felt grumpy and eons older than his twenty-nine years. The job did that, jaded you and aged you. Josh would learn that soon enough, and because Rand remembered how eager and enthusiastic he'd once been, he felt a pang that he'd lost his joy. And the truth of it was, he couldn't blame that loss on this undercover assignment or even the FBI. But, as he always did when he thought of his daughter, he slammed the lid down on that particular box.

"I'm not grumpy," he grumped.

Josh snorted. "Dude, you so are."

Dude was Josh's new favorite word, one he'd picked up from the Gentrys, and Rand wasn't sure he'd ever forgive the brothers for that. He eyed his fellow agent. Josh had also taken to dressing like the bikers with unholy glee. Decked out in a skintight black Harley-Davidson logoed T-shirt, torn-at-the-knees jeans, heavy motorcycle boots, and chains hanging out of his pockets, he was indiscernible from every other man in the bar, except he smelled better than most.

Proper dress had been ingrained in Rand from childhood. His pressed jeans and ironed T-shirt—that was not skintight—were what the weekend bikers wore. The Harley-riding doctors, lawyers, and CEOs. But whatever. The bikers had taken to Josh as one of the new owners of Aces & Eights from day one, but they didn't know what to make of Rand.

Strangely, that was working to their advantage. The bikers tended to behave when he was around, even watching their language. He wasn't sure what that said about him. Did they think he was a badass like the Gentrys? Rand snorted. Doubtful. However, they were starting to trust Josh enough that they weren't guarding their conversation around him. That left Rand to manage the bar and the customers, while Josh busied himself with ferreting out their secrets.

Rumors were surfacing that the Hot Shots, one of the regular clubs that frequented Aces & Eights, were dealing in guns. "You pick up on any more talk about those weapons?" he asked Josh.

"Nothing more than what I've heard so far, but the Hot Shots are here tonight. They're loosening up around me, letting things slip."

"We can bring Nate up to speed in our meeting tomorrow, see how he wants us to handle this. Just be careful around them."

"Dude, I'm Superspy. They don't suspect a thing."

Rand shook his head, grinning at the kid.

The door opened and a couple walked in, catching Rand's attention. After stepping inside, they came to a stop, taking in their surroundings. They weren't bikers; that was obvious. Nor were they the kind of people who frequented Aces & Eights. In fact, Rand recognized the man, having seen his picture on the sports segment of his local news. Aiden Calloway, a University of Miami linebacker recently drafted by the Miami Dolphins. What the devil was he doing here?

Rand's gaze shifted to the woman, and his heart tripped over itself. She was beautiful with her long black hair and smoky brown eyes. Bedroom eyes, he thought. She was a few inches taller than the average woman, curved in all the right places, and when her gaze landed on him and held, his breath hitched.

Josh whistled. "Nice."

Rand glanced at his fellow agent to see appreciation in his eyes as he looked at the woman. For the first time the kid didn't amuse him. "She's obviously taken." That had come out harsher than he'd intended, considering the puzzled look Josh gave him.

"Doesn't mean I can't admire a beautiful woman," Josh said, then wandered away.

No, it didn't, and whoever she was, she was the first

woman to catch Rand's interest since Olivia. He slipped his hand into his pocket and pulled out Zoe's necklace, the one he'd never had a chance to give her. He stared at the dainty heart with a sapphire gem—her birthday stone—for a moment, then dropped it back into his pocket and turned his back on the woman with the beautiful brown eyes.

His grief was too deep, his heart too dead to do more than manage a day-to-day existence. There was nothing left of him to give any woman. That he'd even noticed the one who'd walked through the door might be an anomaly, but it didn't change anything.

He caught sight of a biker with a badass reputation looming over Spider and sighed as he headed that way. "Snake, if you don't stop picking on Spider, you're gonna be out the door." Christ, these bikers and their stupid names.

Spider grinned like an idiot. "Aw, he's just playing, boss man. Ain't ya, Snake?"

"Sure, dude."

Snake drifted away, and Rand put his hand on Spider's shoulder. The little man loved all the bikers and just couldn't comprehend that his affection wasn't returned. Mostly it was, but not from the president of the Hot Shots. And Snake was as mean as they came.

"That one's not someone you want to mess with, Spider. So do me a favor and stay out of his way. Okay?"

"'Kay. But he don't really mean it, boss man. He just likes people to think he's badass."

It was impossible not to like Spider. With a few exceptions like Snake, the bikers had adopted Spider as their mascot. Somewhere in his late fifties or early sixties, Spider was the most naive and had the kindest heart of anyone Rand had ever met. Barely topping out at five-six, as bald as a billiard ball, and as scrawny as a toothpick, the man was a permanent fixture at Aces & Eights.

One of the things Rand liked best about him was that he

didn't belong to any of the clubs. Spider was just a funny, likable little man who the Gentry brothers had instructed Rand to look out for. Since stepping through the doors of Aces & Eights, Rand had kept Spider in his line of sight but had only had to rescue him for the first time tonight. Damn Snake to hell.

Rand leaned against the bar after Spider walked away, his gaze scanning the room, looking for trouble stirring. He'd learned early on that it was best to put a stop to anything brewing before it boiled over into an all-out brawl.

"She was asking about the previous owners," Josh said, sidling up next to him.

"Who?"

"The gorgeous woman who came in a few minutes ago."

Rand slid his gaze to her. She and her friend were heading for the door. Why would she be asking about the Gentrys? "Follow them, find out where they live."

☾

After Josh returned with two addresses—and why did it please Rand that the couple didn't live together?—it only took a few minutes to have a background report on both of them. Aiden Calloway had one arrest for disorderly conduct, but the charges had been dropped against him and the other fraternity pledges for cavorting naked in a hotel's fountain.

Kinsey Landon had also graduated from the University of Miami at the same time as her friend and now worked as a buyer for Summer Fashions. She'd been raised by a single mother in Jacksonville, Florida. From all appearances, the two had lived a quiet, simple life. Her mother had died last year. Almost twenty-four, Kinsey lived by herself in a ground-floor apartment on the edge of Coral Gables. Not the best neighborhood but not the worst.

She'd qualified for a partial scholarship—enough to cover her textbooks, but probably not much more than that—

and had worked part-time at Summer Fashions until she'd graduated and had been offered the job of junior buyer. She didn't have a record, not even one parking ticket. What she did have was a mountain of student loans to pay off.

"Exactly what did she want to know about the Gentrys?" he asked Josh. Anytime someone was nosy about a federal agent or three, it was wise to pay attention. Especially where the brothers were concerned because of their former undercover work. Even if it was someone as seemingly innocent as Kinsey Landon.

"She wanted to know if the owners were around, and when I told her I was one of the owners, she asked my name. When I told her it was Josh Sheridan, she seemed surprised. Then she asked if I knew anyone with the last name of Gentry. I almost told her no. Then I realized all she had to do was ask just about any of our customers to get a yes. So I told her they used to own the bar but had sold it to me and my partner."

"Anything else?"

"The guy dropped her off at her apartment, didn't go in. Then I followed him to his place. Why do you think she'd be asking about the brothers?"

"That's the question, isn't it?"

"We should tell them."

Rand thought about it for a moment. "No. Don't say anything yet. It's probably nothing, in which case, she doesn't need the brothers' attention on her."

"I know I wouldn't want their attention on me," Josh muttered. "She seemed nice, so maybe she just heard about them and wanted to see them for herself. They're like a legend, you know."

"Yeah, that's probably it." Rand smiled at the baby agent. He was still too trusting, but he'd learn. For now he'd prefer that Josh forgot about Kinsey Landon until Rand could get a handle on why she was asking about the Gentrys.

"Go keep an eye on the animals. I'll be out in a few

minutes."

"On it, dude."

After Josh closed the door behind him, Rand logged in to the security cameras, and when he found the sequence where Kinsey and Aiden entered, he watched it through several times. Something about it was nagging him. It was on his fourth time of viewing it that it hit him. They weren't a couple, not in the sense that they were boyfriend and girlfriend. Their hand-holding wasn't natural, nor did she look at Aiden like a woman in love or on the way to love. Her friend was protective of her but more in a brotherly kind of way. That shouldn't please him, because Olivia had taught him to avoid beautiful women like the plague.

❧

Where the devil were her keys? Kinsey scanned her desktop where she usually dropped them when she arrived each morning. She scooted her chair back and looked around the floor. Nope, not there.

"Kinsey, the girls need some help out on the floor," Corrie, her boss and the senior buyer, said. "We're kicking ass with this sale."

"Coming." She'd have to look for her keys later. They had to be around here somewhere.

It was almost closing time, and she was still on the sales floor. There were only two women in the store now, both in the fitting rooms trying on clothes. Kinsey was tidying up around the register while the sales consultants refolded clothes and straightened racks. Corrie hadn't been kidding. They'd killed it today with this buy-one-get-one-half-off sale. She groaned when Sebastian Summer sauntered in, a smirk on his face as he headed straight for her.

She tensed, gritting her teeth when he not so accidently brushed his hand across her butt when he stopped behind her. He'd been doing that more and more lately, and she could no longer ignore it, even if it meant losing her job.

She turned, pressing her back against the counter. "Do that one more time, and I'll file a sexual harassment report."

It was a weak threat, considering his father owned the five Summer Fashions stores scattered around Miami. Daddy turned a blind eye when it came to his only child. She loved her job as a junior buyer for the stores, had been thrilled that she'd found a position where she could put her degrees in fashion and business management to good use. Corrie had warned her of Sebastian's roving hands, but Corrie's advice on what to do about it pretty much sucked.

"Just let him have his fun. He's harmless," Corrie had said on Kinsey's second day after Sebastian had pressed his elbow against her breast, letting it linger there.

Well, he might be harmless—although she had her doubts about that—but he wasn't going to have his fun with her. "I'm not kidding, Sebastian," she said when he smirked. "Touch me one more time and I'll report you."

He shrugged.

Yeah, that had been an empty threat. She could go to the labor board, or whichever government department she could file a harassment complaint with, but that would definitely make it impossible to stay at Summer Fashions. She doubted she could find another job as good as this one, but if Sebastian pushed her too far, she'd have no choice.

"So you and me, drinks tonight?"

The man was honest-to-God certifiable. After telling him she'd file a report on him, he had the nerve to think she'd go out drinking with him?

She waved a finger between them. "You and me, so not happening, tonight or any other night." Asshole.

He smirked. "We'll see."

The bell over the door dinged, signifying that someone had entered the shop. Out of the corner of her eye, she saw a man stop and say something to Shannon, one of the sales girls. Then he headed her way. When she tried to step away to take care of the customer, Sebastian grabbed her arm, digging his fingers into her skin. "You like your job here?"

"Very much, and because I do—"

"Can you help me pick out a gift for my mother? Today's her birthday, and I want to get her something nice."

Kinsey looked into the face of the man from Aces & Eights... the drop-dead gorgeous one. She didn't believe in coincidences, didn't believe he'd randomly walked into the one store in Miami where she worked.

He slid his gaze to Sebastian, then down to the fingers still digging into her skin, his eyes going cold. "You're going to leave bruises on her arm, man."

Sebastian took his time letting go. "We'll talk later, doll." He gave her his signature smirk before walking through the doorway to where their offices were located.

"He a problem?"

What did he care? "He's the boss's son. He's allowed to be a problem."

"Makes for a sticky situation then."

Truth. "Are you really looking for a present for your mother, man from Aces and Eights?"

A wide smile appeared on his face, one that reached his blue eyes, making them crinkle at the corners. "Ah, so you remember me."

"Vaguely." Ha! Like she could forget. Their eyes meeting across the room at the bar had been right out of a romantic movie, the kind of moment where it felt like time stopped. Well, for her, anyway. She doubted he'd thought twice about her after she was out of his sight. She'd sure thought of him, though. More than she'd liked. Her hands itched to muss up his golden-blond hair, and she wanted to press her fingers against the sinewy muscles that his bar T-shirt had failed to hide.

One thing she'd noticed was that he was clean-shaven, unlike the scruffy faces of the men she'd seen in the bar. It was a look that totally worked for him. His features were both elegant and strong. And those lips… full and sensual, a mouth made for kissing.

There were other things that seemed different from the hard-core bikers. She was an expert on clothes, and his were expensive. And then there was the Breitling watch. Although not flashy, the price tag would have been way out of her league. Who was this man who hung out in biker bars but looked and dressed like a GQ model?

"Rand Stevens," he said, holding out his hand.

She stared at that hand, afraid that if she touched it, she would combust or something just as messy. "Um, Kinsey." Not wanting to be rude, she put her hand in the one he still held out. And whoa! Delicious tingles raced merrily up her arm. His eyes widened as if he felt them, too. Time had a way of stopping around this man, and that unsettled her.

"So, your mother?" She tugged her hand free.

"Yes, Kinsey, I really do need a present for my mother." He glanced around the store. "I was actually headed for Galleria but saw a beautiful scarf in your display window that would be perfect for her."

So he hadn't known she worked here. That was a relief since it meant he wasn't stalking her. "I know the one you're talking about. It's an original, hand-painted by a local artisan. It's pretty expensive," she said, not wanting him to be embarrassed when he saw the price.

He grinned. "Only the best for Mom."

Okay, silly her. If he could afford a Breitling watch, a mere scarf costing a few hundred was obviously no big deal. "I'll get it for you." She could feel his gaze on her back as she walked to the display window, and it unnerved her in a good kind of way. Her back heated as if a fire burned in his eyes, and her legs suddenly felt as wobbly as a baby's when learning to walk. Don't trip. Don't trip. Don't trip.

She managed to retrieve the scarf and return without

falling on her face, a true miracle. Maybe she should start wearing flats from now on for when hot men wandered into the store to buy presents for their mothers, since that was apparently a lethal combination.

"Do you want it gift wrapped?" And just listen to her voice getting all husky. It was embarrassing.

"If it isn't a bother, Kinsey."

She wished he wouldn't say her name in that panty-melting way. He followed her over to the gift-wrap station.

"Fate is at work here."

"How so?" She glanced over her shoulder at him, her fingers getting tangled up in tape at seeing the way he was looking at her. As if he wanted to eat her up. Well, that was only fair. She very much wanted to devour him. Wanting to be naughty with a man she'd just met wasn't her... well, it never had been before now.

"Seeing that scarf in the window and detouring into this store. Finding you here. I've thought about you a lot since the night you walked into the bar. Go out with me, Kinsey. Breakfast, lunch, dinner, drinks, or just for coffee. Take your pick."

"I don't date bikers." She might make an exception for him, though.

"I've never been on a bike in my life. Those things scare the hell out of me."

She taped a bow onto the wrapped box. "Then what were you doing at a biker bar?"

"I'm one of the owners."

That got her attention. "You don't think that's weird? Owning a biker bar when you're afraid of motorcycles?" Would he know her brothers?

Amusement lit his eyes. "Very much so."

"Sounds like there's a story there."

"Go out with me, and I'll tell you how that came about."

"Are you a serial killer?"

"That would be a no."

"Okay. Lunch. I'm off on Sundays and Mondays. And I'll meet you wherever you pick." She wouldn't pass up a chance to find out if he knew her brothers, but it was more than that. All this man had to do was look at her with those blue eyes and she was ready to agree to anything he asked.

"Sunday. You have your phone on you?"

She pulled it out of her jacket pocket. He gave her his phone number, and after she'd put it in her contacts, he said, "Now call me so I'll have yours."

Numbers exchanged, she headed to the register. "See you Sunday," she said after he paid.

"I'll be counting the minutes until then."

Heavens, his smile was lethal. She waited until he walked out before saying, "Me, too."

When she finally returned to her cubicle, dog-tired and wishing she was already soaking in the bubble bath on her agenda for tonight, she saw the tip of her keys sticking out from under a folder. She frowned. How had she missed seeing them there?

CHAPTER THREE

"IF IT ISN'T THREE OF the ugliest brothers to walk the land," Rand said upon entering the field office's conference room and seeing Nate, Court, and Alex Gentry sitting at the table.

Alex snorted. "You just wish you had half our good looks, dude."

"And that's another thing." He slid into the seat next to Court. "All three of you are on my shit list for teaching Josh that word. If he calls me 'dude' one more time, I'm going to duct tape his mouth shut."

That got a full-bellied laugh from Alex, a laugh from Court, and a chuckle from Nate, which about summed up the personalities of the brothers. Alex saw the fun in everything, Court sometimes did, and Nate rarely. Rand did have to concede that since Nate had finally gotten out of his own way and admitted that he loved Taylor Collins—one of their fellow agents—the man actually smiled these days.

"Dudes! Sorry I'm late," Josh said, almost tripping over his own feet as he rushed in.

Rand coughed down a laugh, but Alex didn't even try. Both Nate and Court chuckled, amusement in their eyes as they watched Josh scramble for a seat.

He scrunched his eyebrows together. "What'd I miss, a good joke?"

"Dude," Alex said, his lips still twitching, "we were just talking about all the ways to use duct tape."

Rand groaned. "Let's get this meeting started." Before Alex decided it would be fun to tell Josh one of those uses. They spent an hour discussing what they knew so far on the Hot Shots, which wasn't much. Mostly just rumors that they were dealing in stolen weapons. They were a new club at Aces & Eights, one the Gentrys hadn't dealt with during their time at the bar. After giving Josh the approval to dig deeper, Nate ended the meeting but told Rand to stay behind.

"You aren't comfortable at Aces and Eights, are you?"

With any other boss Rand would have assured him otherwise, but with Nate he knew he could be honest without repercussions. "It's not so much that I'm uncomfortable as that I don't fit in. The bikers are never going to warm up to me."

Nate leaned back in his chair and tapped his finger on his lips. "The problem is that you're not meant to work undercover."

"Or this is just the wrong undercover job for me."

"The thing is, a good undercover cop or agent can fit into whatever the operation is, and most of those involve the seedy side of life. You don't know what to do with the dark side."

So he was a disappointment. "I… I'm—"

Nate waved a hand at him. "There's no reason to apologize. You're a damn good agent. We just need to get you back to doing what you do best. I'm working on getting someone transferred to this office to take your place at the bar, but until that happens, you're going to have to stick it out. Someone needs to keep an eye on Josh."

"You know I will." The relief that coursed through Rand surprised him. Until now he hadn't admitted, even to himself, how unhappy he was with his assignment. "Josh is doing a great job. He just needs to settle down a little."

"I know. While I appreciate his enthusiasm, his eagerness to prove himself could get him in trouble."

That was true, and he'd never forgive himself if something happened to the kid. "He'll settle down soon enough. Anything else?"

"No. I think we've covered everything."

He almost told Nate about Kinsey Landon but decided to hold off. The more he learned about her, the harder it was to see her as a threat. It was true what he'd told Josh. Having any of the Gentrys' attention on you was the last thing you'd want.

Until and unless she proved otherwise, he'd consider her innocent of any harmful intentions. He swallowed his discomfort for misleading her, although he'd mostly told her the truth. The scarf had been a birthday present for his mother. He just hadn't mentioned said birthday was three months away. And he had been thinking of her since the night he'd first seen her, even though he hadn't wanted to.

As Rand drove home to change into jeans and a T-shirt before heading to Aces & Eights, he thought about what Nate had said. It was true. He didn't know how to act around the people who frequented Aces & Eights. Until he'd become an FBI agent, the dark side of life hadn't touched him. And he didn't include losing his daughter in that. That hadn't been the kind of dark that Nate was talking about.

From the day he'd been born, Rand had the best. The best clothes, the best schools, meals cooked by a world-class chef. His first car had been a BMW—given to him as soon as he was licensed to drive—and his friends had all been like him. Privileged.

Was he grateful that he hadn't known hunger or had to worry if he would have a place to sleep at night? Hell, yes. Did he feel guilt that he was privileged by birth? Yeah, he did. His first glimpse of how it would be to wonder if he'd have enough money to even buy a cheap hamburger had been in his first year at Yale. His roommate had attended on a full scholarship, a boy with a brilliant mind.

Unlike Rand, everything had been against Tyrone from his first breath. A drug-addicted mother, a nonexistent father, in and out of foster care, and that was just for a start. Yet Tyrone had somehow believed in himself, had managed to avoid the drug scene, and through hard work and study had landed a full scholarship at one of the most prestigious schools in the country. Against all odds, they'd become best friends, the rich boy and the boy who'd moved into Rand's dorm room with only two pairs of cheap pants and three white dress shirts with the Walmart tags still on them.

Tyrone had both impressed him and fascinated him. Despite not having much in common, they'd eased into being friends. Tyrone was funny, and his impersonations of classmates and celebrities would have Rand laughing so hard his stomach hurt. Over time they'd opened up to each other, learning they had one important thing in common that brought them even closer. Neither one of their mothers put her son first in her life. Rand's cared more about her social life and impressing her peers, and drugs came first for Tyrone's.

Rand's major was business and economics, and he would go to work for his father as soon as he graduated. Tyrone's major was criminal justice. He wanted to join the FBI, often talked about doing his part to make the world a better, safer place.

Then near the end of their first year Tyrone's mother had called, panicked because she owed a dealer money that she didn't have, and the dealer had threatened to kill her. She had a brother who lived in Philadelphia who'd agreed to let her stay with him for a while, and Tyrone planned to take her there.

Rand had driven him to the bus station, but he'd had a bad feeling and had tried to talk Tyrone out of going. He'd offered to give Tyrone the money to wire to his mother, but his friend had refused.

"I won't be able to pay you back," Tyrone had said.

Rand had responded that he didn't have to.

"I'm not your charity case." There had been anger in his friend's voice, so Rand had let it drop, something he would always regret. Two hours after arriving home, Tyrone had been shot and killed, along with his mother.

The world had lost a beautiful soul, a young man who would have made a difference. After hearing about his friend's death, Rand had sat in their dorm room, in the dark, as one question churned in his mind. What kind of difference would he make in the lives of others working for his father, his only goal to make more money? Didn't they have enough? The next day Rand changed his major to criminal justice and, in homage to his friend, joined the FBI after graduation. Although his father had been disappointed, Rand had never regretted his decision.

Life had been great. He had a job he loved and a wife and daughter who were his world. Then his little girl died from the flu. The fucking flu, something he'd never thought to worry about. One day she'd been fine, the next morning feverish, and two days later she was gone.

His marriage hadn't survived the heartbreak, and he'd lost everything important to him. The breakup of his marriage had hurt, but he could recover from that. It was losing his daughter that he couldn't come back from.

☾

On Sunday Kinsey followed the hostess through the restaurant. As soon as Rand saw them approaching, he stood. He was dressed in a blue button-down—the sleeves rolled up—and black pants. His eyes tracked her approach, and he had that killer smile on his face. What else was a girl's heart to do but flutter at the sight of him looking sexier than any man should?

"You look lovely, Kinsey," he said as he pulled out a chair for her.

"Thank you." If you melt in a puddle at his feet, Kins, I'll never forgive you.

She'd spent an hour trying to decide what to wear, finally choosing a white sundress and white strappy sandals. The all white against her olive skin and dark hair was an eye-catching contrast, and the outfit was sexy without being trashy. Based on the appreciation in his eyes, he liked her choice.

"This is nice." She glanced around the room. "I've never been here before." Lush green plants in pots on the floor and flowering plants in hanging baskets gave the place a tropical atmosphere. The tablecloths were pale rose, the floors a rich, dark wood, and the large window next to their table framed a spectacular view of the Atlantic Ocean.

"I'll admit that I was half-afraid that you'd cancel."

She peered over the top of her menu. "Would you have been disappointed if I had?"

"Heartbroken." He tapped two fingers over his heart.

"Then it's a good thing I'm here. I'd hate to know I was the reason for your broken heart." Every time his lips curved up in a smile that was just short of wicked, she wanted to sigh. He was dangerous. To her, for sure.

Their waiter appeared. "What can I get you to drink?"

"Kinsey?" Rand said. "Would you like a glass of wine?"

"A pinot grigio would be nice."

"A club soda with lime for me," Rand said.

"What's good here?" she asked after the waiter left.

"Everything. I particularly like the salmon with the citrus glaze, but their beef dishes are also very good."

She set down her menu. "The salmon sounds great." They chatted about the view and the hot weather for a few minutes until the waiter returned with their drinks.

Rand ordered the salmon for both of them, and when they were alone again, he said, "Tell me something about Kinsey Landon."

"Not much to tell. I recently graduated from the University of Miami. I worked part-time for Summer Fashions my last two years of school, and after graduation they offered me the position of junior buyer. That's about it."

"I have a feeling there's much more to you than that. What do you like to do for fun?"

She shrugged. "Haven't had much time the last few years for play, what with working my way through college."

"Unacceptable. You're too young not to have some fun in your life."

"Maybe you could show me how to have fun." He was easy to talk to, and she really liked that.

"I could maybe do that."

There was a promise in his eyes, one that sent a shiver down her spine. To try to cool the heat building inside her, she took a drink of the chilled pinot and then sighed with pleasure. "This is delicious. Crisp with perfect hints of lime, lemon, and green apple."

He raised a brow. "You know your wines."

Pleased that he picked up on that, she smiled. "I'm learning. I joined a wine club last year. We meet once a month and focus on one wine or sometimes a particular winery. It's fun."

"See, I knew you were holding out on me."

"If I tell you all my secrets right up front, you'll get bored with me." *Like I have three brothers you might know.*

"I seriously doubt that."

The waiter delivered their meals, and Kinsey took a moment to appreciate the presentation. A thick piece of salmon glistening from the glaze sat on a bed of fresh greens, surrounded by grilled asparagus on one side and roasted red potato halves on the other.

"This is too pretty to eat," she said and then grinned. "But I'm going to anyway." Money had always been tight for her and her mother, and they'd never dined in a restaurant of this caliber. Her usual lunches were yogurt or ready-to-microwave soups. She intended to enjoy every bite.

"Your turn. Tell me about Rand Stevens and how you came to own a biker bar. I'm having trouble seeing that one."

"I blame Josh for that. He's like a brother to me, and he was determined to buy the place when it went up for sale. I pretty much agreed just so I could keep an eye on him. Keep him out of trouble. It's a rough crowd, as you saw for yourself."

His reason didn't quite ring true, but she couldn't put her finger on why. Maybe because he just didn't look the part. She took a bite of her salmon, closed her eyes, and moaned. "Oh God, this is so good."

"Don't do that."

She lifted her gaze to his. "What?"

"Close your eyes and moan."

"Ah, that." She took another bite and moaned, then said, "Oops."

He laughed, but the heat in his eyes could start a bonfire. "I love a woman who enjoys her food, but you're killing me, Kinsey."

Good, because he was slaying her looking at her like he was. Before he thoroughly distracted her, she needed to ask about her brothers. "Who owned the bar before you and Josh?"

The heat vanished from his eyes, replaced by wariness. Why was that?

"Three brothers. Why?"

"Just curious if they looked more like bikers than you do. Did you ever meet them?" She still wasn't sure she wanted her brothers to know about her. If she told Rand her reason for asking, he might tell them about her.

"Once, when we closed on the bar, and yes, they looked like bikers."

He was suspicious now, and she didn't want that. "Maybe we should take you shopping, buy you some leathers and chains."

"Chains? That could prove interesting." He waggled his eyebrows.

"Not those kind of chains, silly man. I noticed most of the men in the bar had chains attached to their belt loops that disappeared into their pockets. Weird, huh?" Hopefully she'd distracted him.

"Ah, those. Their wallets are attached to the chains. Keeps them from being stolen."

"Guess they don't trust their friends. Do you have a girl-friend or a wife tucked away? I should have asked you that when you invited me to lunch." But it was hard to think around him.

"An ex-wife and no girlfriend. You?"

"Nope, no wife or girlfriend." She loved making him smile. "Not even a boyfriend."

"I'm happy to hear that. Okay, next question. What're two things you've always wanted to do but doubt you ever will?"

She didn't even have to think about it. "Skydive and attend a fashion show in Paris."

"Interesting choices. One's daring and one relates to fashion, something you love."

"Exactly. Although I'm not sure if I'd have the nerve to jump out of a plane."

"I think you would. Ready to go?"

"Yes. Thank you for lunch."

"My pleasure, Kinsey, believe me."

After he paid, he walked her to her car, keeping his hand on her lower back. Nothing had felt more right... that warmth from his palm seeping into her skin.

At her car door he slipped his hands into his pockets and settled an intense gaze on her. "I'd like to see you again."

"I'd like that, too." And for more than to learn what he knew about her brothers. He was fascinating, a mix of aristocrat, seriously sexy man, and old soul. She'd caught glimpses of pain in his eyes when he let his guard down, and she wanted to know what had put the sadness there. "I'll call you." He leaned down and brushed his mouth over hers. It was a brief kiss, nothing more than a feathering of their lips, but it told her one thing. She wanted more. He waited for her to get in her car, and as she drove away, she watched him in her rearview mirror as he stood, alone in the parking lot.

"You're a mystery, Rand Stevens," she whispered as he faded from sight. "An irresistible one."

Back home, Kinsey grabbed the bag of birdseed at seeing Oscar come to a fluttering stop on her birdbath. As soon as she walked onto the patio, the macaw said, "Hello, pretty."

She smiled. "Thank you, Oscar." He was the pretty one with his red head and tail and his blue wings. She and the bird had become good friends in the last few weeks. "And how is Oscar today?"

"Naughty Oscar," he said in a high-pitched voice that seemed like it should have been coming from an older woman and not a macaw.

He always said that, making her wonder if he'd been such a bad bird that his owner had opened her door and allowed him to fly away. If so, that was just sad. It was obvious that he was used to being taken care of and wouldn't be able to survive on his own. She'd never had a pet growing up. She had always wanted a puppy and would have promised to care for it, but she'd never asked, knowing money was tight. Oscar wasn't the dog she'd longed for, but he was fascinating. Because of her job she was gone all day, so getting a puppy was out of the question. Oscar would do just fine as her pet friend.

She'd watched the classifieds for a lost macaw, but no one was looking for him, nor had anyone who'd responded to her lost-and-found ad been able to tell her his name.

Tomorrow she'd buy a cage and more food. Then she'd lure him into her apartment.

"So, Oscar, I met a man. Want to hear about him?"

CHAPTER FOUR

THAT AFTERNOON RAND ROAMED AROUND his penthouse apartment overlooking Biscayne Bay. He and Olivia had both fallen in love with the place the minute their realtor had walked them inside. They'd made an offer that same day and had moved in a month later.

He'd lived here alone for the past year and had welcomed the solitude. It was his place to hide and miss Zoe. Where he shut out the world, avoiding anyone who wanted to offer him comfort or sympathy. He didn't want their awkward words or hugs or pats on the back. There was no comfort to be found in a world without his little girl.

But something was different today. The space felt too cold, too big for the emptiness inside him. For the first time he was lonely. He didn't want to be lonely, much less thinking of a black-haired, smoky-eyed woman who made him want to join the living again.

For months after Zoe had died and his wife left him, he would come back to this place each night and drink himself into oblivion. At first he was able to hide the extent of his drinking, but eventually it started to affect his performance. The day Rothmire, his boss at the time, called him out on it and gave him an ultimatum—clean up his act or get out—he'd quit cold turkey. As far as his fellow agents knew, he'd dealt with his daughter's death. It was an act, one he'd perfected. He'd never be over it.

He went into Zoe's bedroom, something he used to do every day when he was drinking. Because being in this room—looking at her toys, the bed she'd slept in—sent an instant craving for alcohol straight to his gut, he'd avoided coming in here since getting sober. But today he needed to be close to her.

He sat heavily on her bed and buried his face in his hands. Tears burned hot in his eyes, the ache in his heart a bottomless black hole that would never heal. When the tears dried up, he lifted his head and scanned the room, his gaze pausing on Baby Belle sitting on the dresser. He stood and picked up the doll he'd given his daughter after she'd fallen in love with Beauty and the Beast and had watched it endlessly.

"You're the best daddy in the world," his three-year-old daughter had squealed at seeing the doll, and then she had smothered his face in kisses. He'd sat on this very bed at night, reading her stories to lull her to sleep. Olivia never had the patience to answer their daughter's endless questions about the stories, but he'd loved that special time with Zoe. He smiled, remembering how inquisitive her mind was.

Did Piglet and Tigger live with Pooh, Daddy? Pigeons can't really drive a bus, can they, Daddy? Can I have a cat so he can wear a hat, Daddy?

Realizing he was smiling, he reached up and touched his mouth, confirming his lips were curved up. It was the first time he'd smiled when remembering his little girl since her death.

❧

That evening, restless in his too quiet home, he picked up his phone, and before he could talk himself out of it, he sent Kinsey a text.

R U home

He only had to wait a minute for an answer.

Yes

Can I call you

Sure

"Hey," he said when she answered.

"Hey, yourself."

"I was thinking about you, and ..."What did he want to say? That he'd smiled for the first time when remembering Zoe and wanted to share what a miracle that was? She didn't even know he'd had a daughter. "Just that. Have a nice evening, Kinsey."

"Are you okay?"

It wasn't like him to let his emotions show in his voice. "I'm fine. I shouldn't have—"

"If you told me you had a loaded pizza ... well, excluding olives, I might invite you over."

He smiled. "You have something against olives?"

"Yes. And I don't know anyone who likes anchovies, so it should be a given that those are a no, too."

His smile grew wider. "No anchovies. I don't get your aversion to olives, but I'm with you on the stinky fish things."

"So, are you saying you have a loaded pizza?"

"I absolutely am."

"Then bring that thing over. It beats the frozen dinner I was going to nuke in the microwave."

That brought on a grimace. He'd never eaten one of those in his life. They couldn't possibly taste much better than eating cardboard. "Text me your address. I'll be there in an hour." He congratulated himself on thinking to ask for her address even though he knew it.

After hanging up, he called his favorite pizza restaurant and placed an order, then took a quick shower. Dressed in cargo pants and a Polo shirt, he headed out to pick up the pizza. He also brought a bottle of wine from home. Although he no longer drank, he kept wine and beer on hand, mostly for the Gentry brothers and their wives on the occasions when they stopped by.

He knew he was skirting a line where Kinsey was concerned, but he couldn't seem to bring himself to care. The first thing he should have done was report to Nate that someone was asking questions about him and his brothers. Although her questions seemed innocent enough, even wanting to know about the previous owners, who'd been undercover when they operated out of the bar, was cause for suspicion.

Yet he just couldn't see her as a bad guy. *And if you're wrong, Stevens?* At best he'd get a stern lecture from Nate, and at worst he'd lose his job. And even knowing that, he still couldn't bring himself to put her on the FBI's radar. Maybe it was stupid reasoning, but he'd smiled over a memory of his little girl shortly after having lunch with Kinsey, and now the two were connected in his mind. Until and unless he learned otherwise, he'd consider her innocent of having ulterior motives.

As he was leaving the restaurant, pizza box in hand, a woman approached the door, and he paused to hold it open for her. A blonde, blue-eyed little girl walked beside her. Rand's breath caught in his throat, and grief sank its claws into his heart. Somehow he managed to nod at the woman when she thanked him instead of letting the door hit her in the face as he made his escape.

Kinsey showered, then slipped on a pair of shorts and a scooped-neck T-shirt. She was having second thoughts about inviting Rand over, but he'd sounded down, and she'd made the offer before thinking better of it. For one thing she was crazy attracted to him, but a biker bar owner wasn't long-term boyfriend material.

All through college she'd concentrated on school, spending her free time working or studying. She'd had a boyfriend in high school, a really nice guy who'd been as clumsy as her the first time they'd made love the night of their senior prom.

After graduation they'd gone their separate ways, her to the University of Miami, and Rick to the University of Central Florida in Orlando. Up until eight months ago they'd still hooked up when their schedules permitted. Although she knew their relationship was slowly fizzling out, she hadn't had the time or energy for dating. She liked Rick, and he was easy in that he wasn't around to need constant attention from her. Seeing him when they could make it happen was convenient, but then he had fallen in love with a girl in one of his classes. She was happy for him, but she missed the intimacy of being with a man.

She was also ready for a relationship, one that had the potential to go somewhere. As an only child with a mother who frequently worked two jobs to keep a roof over their heads and food on the table, Kinsey had often been lonely. So many times she'd wished for a brother or sister to play with. Long ago she'd decided she wanted a big family when she grew up. A home filled with the love between wife and husband and the laughter of children—at least three, but four would be a nice round number.

The doorbell rang, and taking a deep breath, she opened the door to the man with whom she might or might not play tonight. "Ah, that smells so good," she said, getting a whiff of the pizza.

"I aim to please," Rand responded.

Oh, he pleased her all right, in ways he couldn't begin to imagine. One sight of him in a shirt that did a beautiful job of accentuating what looked like a rock-hard chest and broad shoulders and she made her decision. Bring on the playtime.

"Come on in." She led him to the kitchen, which took about six steps. Her apartment was small, the building old. It was well maintained, though, and she loved the high ceilings and crown molding.

"One pizza, no olives or anchovies, as promised," he said, setting the box on the counter. "And I thought you might like a glass of wine to go with it."

She eyed the bottle and almost choked. "Um, that's a hundred-dollar bottle of wine." She glanced at him to see a slight blush on his cheeks, which was darn cute.

"I didn't expect you to know that."

"I told you I belong to a wine club. Just so happens this was a featured wine a few months ago. Is it from your bar?" she asked as she took two wineglasses from the cabinet.

"No, from home. And you only need one glass. I don't drink."

She paused with the goblets in her hands and stared at him. "You're giving me an expensive bottle of wine from your own collection and you don't drink? And on top of that, you own a bar."

He shrugged. "That about sums it up."

"You get more interesting by the minute, Rand Stevens." She grinned. "A real conundrum. So why don't you drink? Are you an alcoholic?" Her friends said she was sometimes too blunt, but she figured that if someone didn't want to answer any of her questions, all they had to do was say so.

"Not exactly." He opened a drawer and peered into it. She liked that he made himself at home. "Where's your bottle opener?"

She reached past him to open the next drawer over, brushing her arm over his. Touching him hadn't been intentional, but the skin-to-skin contact sent a tingle up her arm. Oh yeah, he was definitely doing it for her. She glanced up at him as she handed him the opener to see him looking at her with eyes that seemed to be burning.

He took the corkscrew from her, letting his fingers slide over hers. "Thank you for saving me from a boring night of staring at my TV." His eyes shifted away. "And some other things."

"My good deed for the day." Although she doubted that he spent his nights staring at his TV. All the man had to do was crook his finger at a woman and she'd come running to him. But he seemed off tonight. His last sentence had been said almost in a whisper, as if he were talking to himself. She had the passing thought that he could use a hug, but she let that go. For the moment, anyway.

After he opened the wine bottle, he poured a small amount into the glass, then handed it to her. "Taste."

She brought the goblet to her nose and sniffed, then sipped a little into her mouth, rolling it around on her tongue. "Mmm." She closed her eyes, savoring the taste. "Full-bodied but firm, a hint of oak and berry and notes of tea leaf, and a little on the earthy side. Extremely good."

"I continue to be impressed." He took the glass from her and filled it to the halfway point. "We probably need to heat up the pizza. It took a little longer to get here than I expected."

She turned on the oven. "Does it bother you to be around alcohol?"

"It used to but not any longer." He leaned against her kitchen counter. "To answer your earlier question, after my divorce I decided it would be a good idea to drown my sorrows in booze, dirty martinis being my favorite embalming fluid."

She wrinkled her nose. "Ugh. Olives. Sorry, but I can't be friends with an olive lover."

"Then I'm heartbroken." He put his hand to his chest, over his heart, and blinked puppy dog eyes at her.

Fighting a laugh, she said, "Since you brought pizza and a bottle of amazing wine, I might make an exception for you."

His sad smile morphed into a grin. "I can manage to have an endless supply of pizzas and amazing wine if that would entice you to remove *might* from what you just said."

"No way. If I make you work for my friendship, you'll appreciate it more."

They chatted for a few minutes until the pizza was hot, then took seats across from each other at her tiny pub table. As they talked, he seemed to come out of his funk, if that was what it was.

She picked up a slice, taking a bite off the end, and as she'd done with her first sip of the wine, she closed her eyes, savoring the taste. "My God, this is the best pizza I've ever had."

"Did I mention an endless supply?"

"All I'll admit to is that you're making it easy to forget you're an olive man." He was smiling, but he still had sad eyes. Did he miss his wife, maybe? "How long have you been divorced?"

"A little over a year."

"You must have taken your divorce hard if it caused you to drink too much."

He set down his slice of pizza, stared at his plate for a moment, then lifted his gaze to hers. "No, that wasn't the reason. Our daughter died." His voice trembled, and he cleared his throat. "We didn't handle it well."

"God, Rand, who would handle losing a child well?" She'd known he carried some kind of pain in his heart, but she'd never thought of it being something so tragic. She reached over and put her hand over his. "I'm so sorry." There were no words adequate to comfort anyone who'd lost someone they loved. She knew that for a fact. And a child? That had to be the hardest loss.

"Her name was Zoe. She died a month before her fourth birthday." He stood, picked up his plate and took it to the sink, then turned, leaned against the counter, and shoved his fingers into the pockets of his pants. "Olivia, my wife, couldn't deal with my grief. I wanted to talk about Zoe. She didn't. She said living with me was too depressing, so she found a man who'd never known Zoe, one who had no upsetting memories of her daughter."

"I hope this doesn't offend you, but your ex-wife was a cold bitch."

He dipped his chin as a brief smile curved his lips. "I

know it sounds like it, but not really. Her way of dealing with the pain was to lock it away, pretend Zoe had never existed. I think she was afraid if she didn't that she'd fall in a black hole and never be able to climb out."

"Okay, I get that. Everyone has their own way of dealing with grief." She thought he was being generous toward his ex-wife, though. "But Rand"—she stood and went to him—"anytime you want to talk about Zoe, I'd love to listen to your memories of her."

His eyes held hers for a beat, and then he reached into his pocket and pulled out a necklace. She took it from his hand. It was delicate, a small silver heart with a sapphire stone on a thin silver chain.

"Hers?" she asked.

"I bought it to give to her on her birthday." He shrugged. "Never had a chance."

And now he carried it with him, a link to his daughter. Tears burned her eyes. She handed the necklace back to him and then pressed her face against his chest. "I hurt for you," she whispered.

His arms came around her, pulling her close. He kissed the top of her head. "I don't want you to hurt for me, Kinsey."

"Someone needs to." She pulled away, took his hand, and tugged. "Come with me." She'd already decided she wanted to play, but her feelings for him had turned into something else, something deeper. He followed without a word as she led him to her bedroom.

CHAPTER FIVE

R AND DIDN'T KNOW WHY HE'D cut open his heart, bleeding out his sad story. It might have been Kinsey's tears when he told her about Zoe. Or maybe it had been her touch when she'd put her hand over his, or it could just be that he was ready to talk about Zoe, share his memories of her with someone who cared. Because he could see in her eyes that she did.

She led him to her bedroom, stopping at the edge of the mattress. Her gaze darted from him to the bed and then to his chest. She didn't seem sure of her next step as they stood facing each other.

"Kinsey," he said, his voice sounding rusty to his ears, and in this he was. He hadn't been in a woman's bedroom since his marriage had gone south. He was still raw from talking about his daughter, but he needed what Kinsey was offering. And it wasn't just any woman he wanted, only her. That connection he'd felt the first time he saw her was growing stronger by the minute, and he wasn't sure what to do with that.

"Yeah?"

"Are you sure you want this?"

She peered up at him with those smoky brown eyes of hers. "I do."

He watched her fingers skim over his arm. "Why? Because if you're offering a pity—"

She shook her head. "Don't even say it. That's not what this is."

"Then what is it?" He didn't want her pity, and he especially didn't want a pity fuck.

"This is a man and a woman who are immensely attracted to each other…" She tilted her head, studying him. "At least I think you're attracted to me."

"'Immensely' is a good word."

Her eyes softened, and she smiled. "We're consenting adults, and we have every right to enjoy each other if that's what we want. I don't go around propositioning men, but I've never wanted a man the minute our eyes met across a room. Until you."

"I'm not happily-ever-after material, Kins."

"Not asking you to be." She arched a brow. "Any other roadblocks you want me to obliterate?"

Rand smiled, something he seemed to want to do around her. And those eyes—he could happily drown in them. "Anyone tell you that you have beautiful eyes?"

"Yes. My mother."

"And now me." He put his hands on her hips. "I didn't come over tonight with the intention of sleeping with you, so I'm not prepared."

"Is that something you need to think about?"

"No, I only mean that I don't have a condom." He didn't even own any, something he'd need to correct if they continued to see each other, and he sincerely hoped they would.

"Oh, not a problem. I have condoms covered. Be right back."

She danced away, stopping at the door, glancing over her shoulder at him. "Don't go away."

"My feet are glued to this spot."

She grinned at him, then disappeared. While she was out of the room, he took the opportunity to remove his gun and holster from a pocket of his cargo pants. Federal agents were required to be armed at all times outside of their home, but he didn't want to have to explain why he was carrying. He slipped out of his shoes, pushed the gun and holster as far into one of them as possible, covered it with his socks, then slid shoes and gun under her bed.

She returned with a box in her hand that she held up for his perusal. "I hope extra-large works," she said with a smirk before setting the box of condoms on her nightstand.

"You sound a little too hopeful," he said on a laugh. "Come here." He sat on the edge of the mattress and spread open his legs. When she came to stand between them without hesitation, he put his hands on her thighs just under the hem of her shorts. Her skin was warm and silky, soft under his fingers. He pulled her down onto his lap, curled his fingers around her neck, and lowered his mouth to hers.

For a time he was able to keep the kiss gentle, but it seemed she wanted more. She sighed into his mouth, and he answered with a groan when she swung her leg around and straddled him. He lifted his head and stared at her for a moment, and the desire in her eyes went straight to his groin. She splayed her hand over his chest, and he put his hand over hers, and then his mouth found hers again.

She tugged on his shirt. "Off."

"Yours, too."

They were a flurry of tangling arms and legs until their clothes were a messy pile on the floor. "You're beautiful, Kinsey. You make my heart pound."

"It's only fair." She took his hand and put it on her breast, showing him that hers was wildly beating, too.

He roamed his gaze over her, pausing on breasts that looked as if they'd be a perfect fit for his hands, and he couldn't wait to have those pert nipples in his mouth. Her skin tone was a light brown, and he wondered if she was of Latin descent. Although her high cheekbones suggested American Indian. That was a possibility as Florida was the home of the Seminole tribe. Actually, as he studied her, he realized there was something familiar about her, but exactly what, he wasn't sure.

"Stop staring at me and get busy," she said, wrinkling her nose at him.

"Not my fault you're a feast for a man's eyes." Especially one coming off a dry spell of over a year. He rolled them over onto the bed and smiled down at her when she giggled. Then her eyes locked on his, and he could swear that sparks of fire were dancing in the air between them. She sucked in a breath as she stared up at him, and he could tell that she felt the connection, too.

He skimmed his hand down the curve of her breast, then flicked his thumb across the nipple, watching in fascination as her eyes softened, then fluttered closed. He did it again, and then lowered his mouth to hers. She moaned when their tongues tangled, sending his blood racing south. If he lasted five minutes, it was going to be a miracle. Because he feared that was a distinct possibility considering how long it had been, he took his time giving her pleasure with his mouth and hands.

Her sweetness was intoxicating, and he could get addicted to her taste. He inhaled her scent deep into his lungs, memorizing it. By the time she was begging him to make love to her—because that was what was happening between them—he'd learned every inch of her body. He'd soaked up her sighs and moans when he'd made her come... twice.

"Please, Rand," she said through heavy breaths.

"Yes." He fumbled for the box of condoms with one hand while crashing his mouth down on hers, kissing her hard and deep. He pulled away long enough to rip the condom open with his teeth and roll it on before picking up where he'd left off because kissing Kinsey was his new passion.

She wasn't shy about touching him, and her hands left a trail of fire over his skin as she explored his body. "You have magic fingers, Kins, but I'm going to embarrass myself in a minute if you keep that up."

"I'll take that as a compliment."

"It was meant as one." He moved between her legs and rested on his knees. The picture in front of him—Kinsey with her hair spread over the pillow, those smoky eyes, and the tongue she swept over her lush bottom lip as she stared back at him—was a fantasy he'd never thought to want, but now feared he was going to crave.

She crooked a finger at him, inviting him in, and it was the best invite he'd ever received. "It's been a while, so I'm apologizing ahead of time," he said as he slid into her. She felt too good, and he stilled, closing his eyes in an effort to gain control.

"Stop saying you're sorry." She wrapped her legs around his thighs and pushed, encouraging him to move.

He decided control was overrated. This time would happen fast, but they had all night and he'd make it up to her. She combed her fingers into his hair, and he buried his face against her neck, scraping his teeth along her skin. A shudder rippled through her, and when she moaned, he found her mouth, swallowing a second moan.

Her scent, her taste, the way she perfectly fit him was almost too much. A sensory overload after a year of not knowing the touch of a woman. He found his rhythm, and once she matched his movements, it was as if they'd made love many times before. It had never been like this, this feeling that he'd come home to a beloved place he hadn't known to miss.

She looked up at him with eyes that snared him with the heat in them, and holding her gaze, he increased the pace of his thrusts. She tilted her hips up as if welcoming him, and he was lost. With each stroke into her, she tightened her inner muscles around him, sending him to the edge. And those little sounds she made were driving him crazy.

"Now," she said.

"Now," he echoed. He scraped his teeth over her shoulder as he thrust harder. The urge to mark her, to claim her as his was strong, and to keep from doing just that, he claimed her mouth instead. She arched up, her body going taut, and when she grabbed on to his arms—digging her fingers into his skin as if she needed him to keep her from flying away—the thread of control he'd been barely hanging on to broke.

Sweet Jesus, that was incredible.

"I'm crushing you," he said when he could form words again.

She shook her head against his shoulder. "You're not."

"*Au contraire*, pretty sure I am." He could feel her breasts pushing against his chest as she tried to breathe. Rolling them over, he kept his arms around her so that she wound up spread over him. "There. Better."

"That was…" She lifted her head, meeting his gaze. Mischief danced in her eyes. "Good."

He narrowed his eyes. "Just good? I'll show you good, woman." He tackled her, and her laughter was the sweetest music. After a time of taking turns to find perfect spots on each other's bodies to kiss, he was ready to go again. Unbelievable. She'd somehow turned him into a randy boy.

Not much later she was begging for mercy, and only when she admitted that making love with him was amazing did he relent and give them what they both wanted. She snuggled up to his side, and once his breathing calmed and he could think again, he thought maybe he'd been wrong to think that he would never love again. Not that he loved her or was even sure he might someday, but the contentment settling in a heart he'd thought was dead and the instant connection he'd felt with her gave him hope that his healing had begun.

"Thank you for telling me about Zoe," she said, her voice sounding sleepy.

He'd thought she had fallen asleep, but at hearing her

say his daughter's name, he smiled against Kinsey's hair. He almost let her comment go, but he wanted to share what had happened earlier today. Mostly because he believed Kinsey had helped in a way he couldn't explain.

"This afternoon I went into her room for the first time in months." He wrapped a ribbon of her hair around his fingers. It was like playing with strands of silk. "And for the first time I smiled when thinking of her." He didn't say, *instead of crying and screaming at the universe for taking my little girl away from me.* He also didn't tell her about the episode at the restaurant when he'd picked up the pizza. That wasn't the first time something like that had happened. The sight of a child, especially a little girl, was a reminder of what he'd lost. He avoided children whenever possible.

Kinsey lifted onto her elbow and stared down at this man who was breaking her heart. "It took me a long time to be able to smile when thinking of my mother, but when it happened, it was the best feeling in the world. My memories of her are special, and I wanted to feel happy when remembering our time together."

She leaned down and brushed her lips over his. "I'm glad that's beginning to happen for you. Zoe would want you to smile when thinking of her."

He slid his hand around her neck and pulled her back to him, giving her a kiss that was both gentle and sweet. "Thank you," he said when he let her go.

He could own her heart if he only half tried, but he'd warned her against falling for him, something she best not forget. Still he had shared something precious with her, so she would do the same.

"You wanted to know why I was at your bar."

"Are you going to tell me a bedtime story?"

His grin and the way his eyes focused on her made her tingle, all the way down to her toes. "Sure, I can do that. Once upon a time there was this girl whose father died before she was born, and that always made her sad. Then her mother, whom she loved dearly, died. The girl found a letter her mother had written her, telling her that the father she'd always wished she'd met wasn't real and that she had three brothers. Because the girl had found herself alone in the world after losing her mother, she wasn't sure how to feel about learning she had brothers. Would she like them? Wish she'd never met them? She finally decided to look for them. Then, after months of searching, the girl learned that her brothers owned a bar called Aces and Eights."

Kinsey frowned at the way the warmth in Rand's eyes faded as she told her story. But she'd started it, so she continued on. "After the girl found out who her brothers were, she wasn't sure she wanted to meet them. She worried that they were bad men. So she went to Aces and Eights, hoping to get a glimpse of them. Instead she met you." She'd thought he would be amused by that, but he pushed her away.

"The Gentrys don't have a sister." He left her bed so fast that she wasn't sure what was happening. "What's your game, Kinsey?"

Game? She didn't have a game. "I don't understand," she said as she watched him dress as if the room were on fire and he needed to evacuate immediately. Then she frowned when she realized what he'd just said. "And how do you know what they have and don't have? You said you only met them once at closing."

"I know they don't have a sister." With those parting words tossed over his shoulder, he was gone.

Kinsey stared at the indent in the pillow where Rand's head had lain. She pushed the covers aside, slipped on her robe, and walked into her living room to lock up behind him.

She leaned her back against the door. "What just happened?"

CHAPTER SIX

RAND STOOD AT THE WINDOW of his penthouse apartment and stared out at the night. Instead of seeing the twinkling lights of the boats, he saw Kinsey's face as she'd told her made-up story. She was a good actress. He'd give her that. She'd looked genuinely confused when he'd said the Gentrys didn't have a sister.

What did she hope to gain by inventing such a tale? Did she think she could just show up out of the clear blue and convince the brothers that they had a long-lost sister? Like they'd fall for that.

And why, when he finally felt a connection with a woman, did it have to be her? *What if she's telling the truth?* He tried to ignore the voice in his head. Her story was just too far-fetched to be true. Wasn't it? But hadn't he thought there was something familiar about her? He closed his eyes and visualized her face; the almost-black eyes, her high cheekbones, and her full lips. It was impossible to deny that they were Gentry features. He'd been so infatuated with her that he hadn't seen what was right in front of him.

"I'm a dead man," he muttered. He'd slept with her. If it turned out she really was their sister, the brothers were going to kill him. First thing in the morning he was going to have to tell Nate about her, and that was one meeting he wasn't looking forward to.

☾

"Got a minute?" Rand asked from the doorway to Nate's

office.

Nate glanced over the top of his monitor. "Of course." He pulled off a pair of reading glasses.

"Didn't know you wore glasses." Rand settled in a chair in front of Nate's desk.

"That happens when you start getting old. Things go to shit." He smirked. "But Taylor thinks I look hot with them on, so there you go."

Rand chuckled. "That's all that counts." Nate and Taylor, a fellow agent, had fallen in love and then married a few months ago. In Rand's opinion Taylor was the best thing that had ever happened to the boss.

"What's on your mind?"

Rand hesitated. If there wasn't a chance in hell that Kinsey was some kind of long-lost sister and he put her on the Gentry brothers' radar, that could cause her a lot of trouble. Should he have told her first that he knew the Gentrys before coming to Nate?

"Whatever's making that smoke pour out of your ears, just spit it out before your brain burns to a crisp."

Right. Just spit it out. "Is there any chance you might have a sister you don't know about?"

Rand had expected a laugh or maybe a snort from Nate. What he got was Nate's full-blown attention, and was that hope he saw in the man's eyes?

"Why are you asking?"

"Because I think I've met her." *And slept with her.* "If you actually have one, that is."

Nate pushed the button on his intercom. "Court. Alex. Get in here. Now!"

Well, hell. They did have a sister and they knew it. It was going to be a miracle if he left this office alive, or at the very least without a black eye or two.

"Dude," Alex said on seeing him. "That was his boss voice." He smirked. "I just hope you're the one in trouble and not me."

Oh, it was going to be him all right.

"Rand just informed me that he's met our sister," Nate said after his brothers were seated.

Alex shot up from his chair. "Where is she?"

If he told them, they'd be on her doorstep in ten minutes flat. The brothers were intense, strong-willed men. He needed to prepare her, especially since she hadn't been sure she wanted to meet them. He wasn't going to stand by and let them overwhelm her with their attentions. Because they would.

"Who is she?" Court asked.

Alex paced in front of him. "I don't care who she is. I want to see her." He glared at Rand. "Now."

"Her name is Kinsey, and—"

"Last name?" Nate said.

"And she thinks the three of you are biker gang dudes, so she's not sure she wants to meet you."

Nate narrowed his eyes, apparently realizing Rand was stalling. "We'll set her straight on that."

"Kinsey," Alex said. "I like that name."

"How do you know so much about her?" Court glanced at Nate. "What's he not telling us?"

That I felt a connection the moment our eyes met. That I slept with her. "Look, this woman came into Aces and Eights—"

Alex made a growling sound. "She came into the bar alone?"

And there was the protectiveness Kinsey would get from her brothers and would hate. Or so he thought. She'd been on her own, making her own decisions for a long time, and it was going to be an adjustment for her to have three very alpha males wanting to dictate her every move. That was the way the Gentrys rolled when it came to those important to them, and Kinsey would be. He doubted if she had a clue how much her life was about to change.

They would mean well, but they'd smother her if she let them. She was a strong-willed woman, though, and it was going to be interesting watching their relationship play out. If he was still alive to see it.

"I don't like that smile on your face, Stevens," Nate said.

So now he was Stevens. And he hadn't realized he was smiling, but he tended to do that where she was concerned.

Court scowled. "I don't either. You better not be messing around with our sister."

"Christ, you three haven't even met her yet, and already you're making decisions for her." Before this little meeting ended up in a brawl, he said, "She's nervous about meeting you. Let me prepare her." It was time to get out of Dodge. He stood. "I'll call you and tell you where she'll be. I won't bother her at work, though, so it won't be until tonight."

He'd made it to the door when Nate said, "Fine, but I better not find out that you're sleeping with her."

That horse already left the barn.

♣

Rand wasn't sure what time Kinsey got off work, so a little before five, he parked outside her apartment. While he waited for her, he called Josh.

"Listen, something's come up, and I'm going to be late getting to the bar."

"No problem, dude."

"It's possible I might not get there at all, but I'll keep in touch. If anything comes up, call me."

"Got it covered, dude."

"Thanks, *dude*," he said, grinning. After he disconnected, he checked his e-mail while he waited. A little before six Kinsey pulled up next to him. He got out of his car and walked to her door. Her frown at seeing him wasn't a surprise considering the way he'd left her last night.

"Rand?" she said after exiting her car.

Distracted by how sexy she looked in a crisp white blouse—unbuttoned just enough to show a tantalizing hint of cleavage—a black pencil skirt, black heels, and her hair pulled back in a low ponytail, he didn't answer her. He needed his mouth on hers, and the urge to back her up against her car door almost—

"Why are you here, Rand?"

"Ah." He blinked away the fantasy playing in his head. "Right. We need to talk." He hated seeing her expression close up and the way her beautiful eyes blanked, especially knowing he was the reason for it. He'd as much as called her a liar when she'd claimed the Gentrys were her brothers.

"Can we go inside?"

She glanced from him to her apartment door as if debating her answer, then shrugged. "Okay."

Rand followed her up the sidewalk but kept a few feet between them. If he was close enough to touch her, he doubted his hand would obey his command to stay at his side. The problem with being behind her was that he had an excellent view of her fine ass and his eyes were drawn to the sway of her hips as she walked ahead of him.

He'd suffered a loss that no parent should have to live through, and he'd shut down, going through his days like a programmed robot. But this woman had him wanting to feel human again. If he could have one wish, it would be to live the previous evening over again, to believe Kinsey when she'd said the Gentrys were her brothers.

Kinsey was mad at her heart for the way it had pounded against her chest when she'd seen Rand waiting for her. He'd hurt her when he'd walked out the way he had. She'd spent the day convincing herself that it didn't matter because he meant nothing to her... Well, when she wasn't avoiding Sebastian's roving hands. He'd been a bigger pest than usual. It was becoming obvious that she needed to look for another job, and that only added to her sour mood.

She almost asked Rand if he wanted something to drink but then decided she wasn't feeling all that cordial toward him. "Well?" she said, turning to face him. The sooner he told her whatever he came to say, the sooner he'd leave. Then she could get about the business of feeling sorry for herself.

He glanced into her living room. "Can we sit down?"

She sighed. "Okay." Ever the gentleman, he waited until she was seated on the sofa before he took the chair next to her.

"First, I owe you an apology, Kinsey."

No kidding.

"I should have believed you. There are reasons for why I reacted the way I did, which you'll understand after you meet your brothers."

What was he saying?

"I do know them, but they'd never once mentioned that they had a sister."

"They don't know." He knew them? Why had he claimed not to?

"Actually, turns out they did, and they've been looking for you."

It was a good thing she was sitting down since she was pretty sure her heart stopped beating.

"Are you okay?" he asked when she put her hand on her chest.

"I don't think so. Did you tell them about me?" At his nod she said, "I told you I wasn't sure I wanted to meet them."

"They're good men, Kinsey. I promise. I know you have questions, and everything will be explained. After they tell you who they are, I hope you'll understand why I doubted you. Then I'm hoping you'll forgive me." He stared at his shoes for a moment, then lifted his eyes to hers. "You're the first woman I've been with since my life fell apart, and you made me feel alive again. I don't know how things will change for you after you meet your brothers or if it's a good idea for us to see each other, but I'd like to if I haven't screwed things up with you."

She'd like that, too, but she wasn't ready to trust him again, so she decided not to commit to anything until she understood why he'd as much as called her a liar. "I guess now that they know about me, I don't have a choice in meeting them." Rand had also taken that away from her. Why hadn't he told her first before going to her brothers?

"No, you don't. If I don't bring you to them, they'll show up on your doorstep." He glanced around her small living room. "They have a strong presence. It might be better to meet them at a neutral location, someplace where you have more space if you decide you need it."

"Let me think about it. Maybe sometime next week." Or next year.

He smiled as he shook his head. "Tonight. They won't wait."

"It's too fast." What did a week or two matter to them? They'd gone this long without her in their life.

"I think my place would be good, and anytime you're ready to leave, I'll bring you home."

"Do I have a choice?"

"You have about an hour before you have three men with strong personalities on your doorstep."

"Fine. Give me a minute, and then we can get this over with."

"I'll wait outside." He took his phone out, and she assumed he was going to call one of her brothers.

She went into her bedroom and retrieved her mother's letter. She paused at the door and pressed her forehead against the frame. Between her feelings for Rand and knowing she was on the way to meet her brothers, she was a hot mess of nerves.

"Mom, look what you've started. I hope you know what you were doing."

☾

Kinsey watched Rand slip a key card into a slot and

then punch the button for the top floor. She was beginning to suspect that her image of a biker bar owner's one- or two-bedroom bachelor pad had missed the mark. A paycheck-to-paycheck man did not live in a luxurious complex right on Key Biscayne. The lobby alone would be a dream to live in with its gleaming black marble floors, white leather chairs and couches, and flower arrangements that must have cost six months of her salary.

When the elevator stopped, they stepped into a foyer with the same black marble floor as in the lobby. There were only two doors, and he put his hand on her back, leading her to the one on the right. Lord, he had half of the entire top floor?

He punched a series of numbers on a keypad, then opened the door. She stepped inside and barely managed to stifle a gasp. One wall was all glass with a view of the bay that had to be magnificent in the daytime. The floor was a beautiful dark wood, the cathedral ceiling soared up, and the walls were painted a soft dove gray. His furniture looked brand-new. The dark gray sofa was massive, but then so was the room. He'd added colors—blues and purples—in the paintings and knickknacks. She smothered a giggle. Calling the pieces scattered around the room knickknacks was insulting them.

She stole a glance at him to see him watching her as if waiting for her reaction, and she got the sense that he was nervous. Why? It was a beautiful home, so was he wanting her to be impressed? She was. He obviously had money. His car was a late model Mercedes, his clothes were expensive, and his home had to have cost a fortune. But he'd never bragged about any of that, which made her think he was afraid she'd like him for his money. A lot of women would. Personally she'd be more comfortable in that bachelor pad that she'd imagined him living in.

"Nice place," she said, making sure she didn't sound like she was gushing. She dropped her purse on the coffee table and then walked to the floor-to-ceiling windows. The view was definitely impressive, one she'd love to see in the daytime. It was pretty now, too. There was a marina below, and some of the boats bobbing in the water had lights on.

He came up beside her, close enough to catch his scent, and she had the urge to nestle her face against his neck and breathe him in. Her brain said to step away, but her body disagreed. She made the mistake of looking up, into his eyes. Something passed between them, something that had her catching her breath. A smiled played on his lips that sent her pulse to racing. She forced herself to put distance between them before she tackled him to the floor and had her way with him.

"When are they supposed to be here? My brothers." The word still felt strange on her tongue.

"Any minute now. Would you like something to drink? A glass of wine?"

"Water would be nice." She'd love to see his wine collection, and maybe she'd get a chance to some other time. Or not. But she wanted to be at her most alert when she met her brothers.

She spied a shelf with photos in silver frames and walked over to it. There was a picture of him with a beautiful little girl who had his blond hair and blue eyes. There was another one of him with his daughter at a younger age. He held Zoe in one arm and his other one was wrapped around the shoulders of a stunning woman who also had blonde hair and blue eyes. Jeez, talk about a beautiful family.

If that was the kind of woman he preferred, what did he see in her? Her mother had been half Seminole, and Kinsey had her features. She'd always been comfortable with her looks, but she couldn't hold a candle to Rand's ex-wife.

"Here you go."

Kinsey glanced at Rand. "Your daughter was beautiful."

He smiled as he looked at the picture she held. "Yes, she was."

"I'm glad you can smile now when talking about her." She set the photo back on the shelf and took the glass of water he held. "Your wife is gorgeous. Do you miss her?"

"No. Not anymore." He put his finger under her chin, lifting her face. "You're the only woman on my mind these days. And Kinsey, in my eyes you're more beautiful than she ever was."

"Thank you." It was hard to stay mad at him when he said things like that. "I've been thinking about you a lot, too."

"Thank God. I was afraid—"

The doorbell rang, sending her heart to skittering. They were here.

"Everything's going to be okay," Rand said, giving her arm a squeeze. He headed for the door.

Nerves were making her palms sweat, and she set the glass on the coffee table before it slipped out of her hand. She started to sit, then thought she should stay standing. Taking a deep breath, her heart beating as if it were a deranged hummingbird flitting around, she waited to see her brothers for the first time.

And good Lord, they were big. They came to a stop a few feet from her. In all her life, Kinsey had never seen such formidable men. The three men standing shoulder to shoulder formed an impenetrable wall, made up of muscle and danger. And they were looking at her.

She'd expected to see them wearing scruffy jeans and biker club vests loaded down with patches, chains hanging from their belt loops. Instead they could have walked off the cover of a men's magazine in their dress pants and button-down shirts. That these three incredibly handsome men were her brothers was surreal.

"It's her," the one in the middle said.

Rand moved next to her, and she slipped her hand into

his, needing his touch to ground her. He squeezed her hand, tightening his fingers around hers.

"She's a lot prettier than us," the youngest-looking one said.

The middle one snorted. "You have a gift for understatement, baby brother."

The oldest was eyeing her and Rand's joined hands, and by his expression he wasn't pleased. Too bad because she wasn't letting go. If she did, she'd probably fall down. Were they as nervous as her? Their faces were unreadable, so she didn't know.

"We've been looking for you," he said. "I'm Nate." He put his hand on the shoulder of the one next to him. "This is Court, and the other one is Alex."

"Rand said you knew about me." Why hadn't they come for her?

Nate nodded. "But only recently, and we have been trying to find you."

"To hell with this," Alex said. He closed the distance between them and wrapped his arms around her. "Hello, little sister," he said. "You have no idea how happy I am that I'm no longer the baby of the family."

Rand let go of her hand when Alex pulled her into a hug. Her first reaction was to grab it back. His hand was her lifeline, the only thing that had been keeping her on her feet. But her brother's arms were strong and welcoming. A brother's embrace was a thing she'd never expected to feel, and she burst into tears.

"Oh hell, she's crying," Nate muttered.

Kinsey laughed against Alex's chest. Her oldest brother had sounded so grumpy, and although she'd only just met them, she sensed that Alex was the easygoing one of the family and Nate the most reserved. If her guess was right—and she couldn't wait to find out, to learn all about them—then that probably put Court somewhere in the middle of the two.

"My turn," Court said, pulling her away from Alex and giving her a hug.

His embrace wasn't as tight as Alex's, nor did it last as long, but his arms still felt good wrapped around her. When Court let go of her, she met Nate's gaze, not sure if she should hug him or what. He was intimidating, and she couldn't begin to read him. Then he smiled and it changed his whole face. Suddenly he wasn't scary anymore. She went to him when he opened his arms.

"I have so many questions," she said after stepping back.

"So do we, but this isn't the place," Nate said. His gaze slid to Rand. "We need some private family time."

Rand looked at her. "Are you good with that, Kins?"

She smiled, liking that he used the same nickname she sometimes referred to herself by. "Why can't we talk here?"

"For one thing our wives are dying to meet you," Court said.

"Yeah, they threatened to not talk to us for a week if we didn't bring you right to them." Alex laughed. "They're nosy creatures and can't stand the thought of being left out."

"All of you are married?" Her brothers nodded. "I had this vision of you as some kind of badass bikers, that you could even be killers. I wasn't sure I wanted to meet you." The men, including Rand, shared amused glances that puzzled her. "What?" she said.

"Not here," Nate said again. "Will you come with us to my house? Our families are there waiting to meet you."

Although they weren't anything like what she'd feared, she didn't know these men and wasn't comfortable just taking off with them.

As if reading her mind, Nate said, "You're safe with us." He sighed when she still hesitated. "Maybe this will ease your mind." He pulled out a black leather case and flipped it open. "Special agent in charge of the Miami field office of the FBI."

CHAPTER SEVEN

R AND SWALLOWED A SMILE WHEN Kinsey's jaw dropped. Now that Nate wasn't working undercover, there wasn't a reason to hide his identity. His picture was, in fact, on their web page as the special agent in charge. He was curious to see how his boss would explain knowing him and Josh.

"I don't understand," Kinsey said. "Didn't you own Aces and Eights?"

"We did and still do," Nate said. "Court and Alex are FBI, too. You couldn't be in safer hands."

Her eyes widened, and then she turned to him. "You, too?"

Unsure how to answer, he raised a brow at his boss.

"He is, but he works undercover. Now forget I told you that," Nate said.

Interesting that Nate was trusting her already.

A smile settled on her face as she eyed him with what seemed like fascination. "I knew there was more to you than you let on."

He winked, getting a bigger smile from her and scowls from her brothers. Their glares brought him to his senses. She was the sister to men he not only worked with but considered friends. The Gentrys would categorically consider the bro code in effect, making their sister off-limits. It was a code every man understood.

They hustled her out; his last sight of her was a glance over her shoulder at him. There was a question in her eyes, one that seemed to ask if she would see him again. He turned away, and when the door closed behind them, he slipped his hand into his pocket, wrapping his fingers around Zoe's necklace. It was a reminder that Kinsey was better off without him.

She was young with a life full of opportunities ahead of her. Someday she'd want to settle down and have a family, and that could never be with him. He would not have another child. He couldn't bear the thought of experiencing that kind of loss again. Better to put the brakes on now before things between them progressed any further. Besides, the Gentrys wouldn't give him a choice in this.

She had brought him back to life, though, if only briefly. Alone again in his home, he went to the window. He noticed Kinsey had left a handprint when she'd stood there looking out, and he placed his palm over the print. It wasn't right to miss something he'd never had. But being with her had helped him realize one thing. Just because he smiled or laughed, it didn't mean he missed Zoe any less.

It was time to join the living again.

C

Rand jogged up the steps to his father's Key Biscayne mansion. He'd called Josh to tell him he would come in tonight after all. On the way to Aces & Eights, Rand's father had called, so he decided to make a quick stop before heading on to the bar.

The first person he came across was the housekeeper. "How are you, Miss Helena?" She'd been with his family since he was a boy, and he adored her. She'd been more of a mother to him than his own. Helena had been the one he'd gone to when he skinned his knee or needed a hug. Although somewhere in her early sixties she was still full of energy.

"I'm not speaking to you, Randall."

She was going to admonish him for not coming around

more often, but he played along. "Tell me what I've done to put that frown on your face so I can immediately make it right."

"You seem to have forgotten how to get here."

"Miss Helena, I could never forget where to come to get my hugs. Now stop making me feel like I'm six years old again and give this old man a little love."

She giggled as she wrapped her arms around him. They both knew why he no longer came to his father's house unless he was summoned. He loved his father and his father loved him. That wasn't in question. But he'd disappointed his father by turning his back on all that he was entitled to, and Harlan Stevens still harbored hope that his son would come to his senses. Rand had tired long ago of the constant pressure from his father to take his place at Stevens Enterprises, and avoided those discussions as much as possible.

As for his mother, she was probably at some thousand-dollar-a-plate charity event. If given the choice of seeing her son or being out with the rich and famous, she'd always pick the latter. But that was old news, something he'd accepted years ago. Her son wasn't her priority. He never had been.

Sometimes when he'd watch the Gentry brothers, seeing the way they loved and supported each other, he'd feel regret that he and his mother didn't have that kind of relationship. For the life of him he couldn't figure out why his father stayed with her, since she didn't give Harlan any more attention than she did her son. Rand figured he could spend an entire year on a psychiatrist's couch and still not get to the bottom of his family's dynamics.

He kissed Helena on the cheek. "Does it help to know that I miss seeing you?"

"Stop molesting me." She swatted his arm but couldn't contain her pleased smile. "Your father's waiting for you in his study. I'll bring refreshments in."

"Do you know what this is about?"

"What do I know? I'm just the housekeeper."

He snorted. Helena knew everything. She could make a lot of money if she ever decided to write a tell-all about one of the richest families in Miami, but she was as loyal to his father as they came. His mother she had no use for, not that he blamed her.

"Stop flirting with my son, Helena, and send him in here," his father said from the middle of the hallway.

Rand winked at Helena, then followed his father to the study. "You should divorce Mom and marry Helena," he said as he took a seat across from the desk.

His dad laughed. "Trust me, I've considered it."

Although it was an ongoing joke between them, Rand wouldn't be at all upset if his parents divorced. They might as well be. His mother lived in one wing of the house and his father in the other. They led their own lives and rarely saw each other, except for the events where she would appear on his arm, seeming to be a loving wife. Regina Stevens liked her husband's money too much to ever leave him, and his father for some reason seemed content with the way things were.

Helena entered, carrying a tray, and Rand stood and took it from her. "Thank you." She smiled, then left, closing the door behind her. After setting the tray on his father's desk, he picked up the cup of coffee and two still-warm chocolate chip cookies. Helena always made those for him when she knew he would be visiting. His father took the crystal tumbler containing the finest scotch whiskey money could buy.

Rand sipped on the coffee that had the exact amount of cream and sugar that he liked. He wondered what Kinsey would think of his father's mansion. She'd thought it was strange that he owned a biker bar but didn't like motorcycles or drink, and he supposed it was. What would she think if she knew just how big his family's bank account was? Between him and her brothers, she'd had some unusual men come into her life. Her reaction when Nate has flashed his badge had been priceless.

"What has you smiling?"

Rand glanced at his dad. "Just thinking of something. You summoned me. I'm here. What's up?"

"I shouldn't have to summon you just to see you."

"If you'd stop trying to talk me into coming to work for you, I'd make an appearance more often." Rand loved his dad but wished he could understand that Rand would never be happy heading up Stevens Enterprises.

His father stared into his glass for a few seconds, then lifted his gaze to Rand. "It was bad enough that you didn't take your rightful place in the company, but pretending to own a biker bar… that is what you're doing, right? Tell me you didn't really buy that place."

Rand was only aware of two people in Miami who seemed to know everything there was to know. One was Nate, the other the man sitting across from him. "You really need to stop spying on me and keep your nose out of FBI business. Yes, I'm working undercover there. It wasn't my choice of an assignment, but you go where you're told."

"Son, I worry every day that I'm going to get a visit from your boss telling me that—"

"And I could walk out your door in a few minutes and get hit by a bus."

"There are no buses on my street." His dad sniffed in distaste.

Rand laughed. "Yeah, well, you know what I mean." He set his empty coffee cup on the table next to him. "I'm as careful as I can be, Dad. The thing is, I love my job." He'd told Harlan this every time the subject of him leaving the FBI came up, but he understood his father's concern.

"And I'm doing something important. Maybe someday I'll decide it's time to quit and come onboard with you, but today isn't it."

"Can you at least ask your new boss… Nate Gentry, is it?" As if his dad didn't know that for a fact. Rand nodded. "Ask him to take you off undercover work? Besides, you're a Stevens, and owning a biker bar, even if it is pretend, isn't good for the family name."

"Since I'm undercover, I doubt it will be a problem." If he admitted that his undercover days were coming to an end as soon as Nate found someone to take Rand's place, his father would start recruiting a replacement for him tomorrow.

"Maybe so, but I don't have to like it."

"No, you don't." Rand eyed his dad. "You didn't ask me to stop by to rehash my employment with the FBI. What's on your mind?"

"I need you to attend the Friends of the Library Ball."

"Because?" Rand braced himself. There was always a reason behind the favors his father asked.

"You're the plus one for Deidre Cummings. And don't even try to come up with an excuse. It's time you crawled out of your hole and started living again, son."

A woman with black hair and smoky brown eyes flashed through his mind. "Funny you should say that. I've been thinking the same thing the last few days. But I don't need you to recruit women for me. I'm capable of finding my own dates."

"Too late. I've already confirmed that you'll escort her."

A prime example of why Harlan was so successful. He just ploughed right through any barriers in his way until he got the results he wanted. "Let me guess. You're either trying to buy her father out, merge with his company, or—"

"The first one, but that's irrelevant. She's a beautiful woman, understands our lifestyle, and would be perfect for you. I'm not asking you to marry her, just go out and enjoy yourself for a change."

"You just described Olivia, and that didn't work out so

well, did it?" His father was conveniently forgetting his own background and the days when he didn't have two coins to rub together. He wondered what Harlan would think of Kinsey.

"It would have if not for…" His dad lowered his gaze for a moment, then lifted eyes that reflected the same sadness Rand lived with every day. "I miss Zoe, too. But it's time to crawl out of your cave, son. You'll take Deidre to the ball, and you will enjoy yourself."

Rand didn't doubt his dad was hurting at the loss of his granddaughter. Even though it was the last thing he wanted to do, the tears in his father's eyes had him agreeing. "Okay. Give me Deidre's phone number. I'll call her and make the arrangements."

"I know you resent my pushing you to do this, son, but I'm only doing it for your own good," Harlan said as he walked Rand to the door. "It's a father's right to worry about his child."

Those last words were as good as an arrow through Rand's heart, the pain intense. He'd worried when they'd rushed Zoe to the emergency room, but it hadn't done a bit of good.

☪

Kinsey glanced over at her passenger. Her brothers hadn't been happy when she'd insisted they make a stop at her apartment so she could get her car. She wanted to be able to leave if she wasn't comfortable. They'd asked so many questions about how safe her apartment security was on the way to her place that she hadn't even gone in. She wasn't ready for them to invade her space, so she'd gone straight from their car to hers with Alex in tow.

So far he was the brother she was the most comfortable with. She couldn't help wondering what her life would have been like if she'd grown up with them.

"What has you so deep in thought, little sister?" He

grinned at her. "I really like saying that."

"Guess you're not the baby anymore," she said, avoiding his question.

"You have no idea how happy that makes me. They'll have to stop calling me 'baby brother' now."

"Well, on the male side you still are the baby brother."

"Just go and burst my bubble." He let out a dramatic sigh, making her laugh.

"Sorry." She stopped behind Nate's car when they arrived at a gate. He punched in a code, then waved his hand for her to follow him in. A high stone wall hid the grounds from view. "Wow, his house is inside here?"

"Actually, so are mine and Court's."

"You guys live in a compound?"

"Yeah. We've made a lot of enemies. This is safer for our families."

That didn't sound good. She parked next to Nate's vehicle and glanced around as she got out of her car. Three houses were set in a half circle, each on what looked like an acre of land. Security lights flicked on as they walked up the sidewalk. Nate had said they were going to his house, so she assumed the one they were approaching was his. It was a sprawling ranch style, and she did a double take at the little faces pressed against the window, watching them.

"Um…"

Alex laughed. "I should warn you that there's a crowd here, waiting to meet you."

Nate opened the door, then stepped aside, motioning her to enter.

"Like how big a crowd?" She stepped to the side while he closed and bolted the door after they were all in. These guys really did seem to take their security seriously.

Alex stared at the ceiling for a second while clicking off his fingers. "Thirteen, plus one Gentry on the way to be exact. Actually, fourteen counting Rosie."

"You're kidding, right?" Were there aunts and uncles she

didn't know about?

"Nope."

He slung an arm around her shoulder, and she couldn't help but like it. I have a family. They entered a large living room, and even though Alex had warned her, she paused at seeing all the people staring at her. I have a really big family. Four of them were women and the rest were children. Wow, her brothers were prolific.

Before she could say anything, three of the women surrounded her, smothering her in a group hug. Kinsey hadn't been hugged by a female since losing her mother, and with her emotions running high at having a family again, she burst into tears, thoroughly embarrassing herself.

"Oh, honey," one of them said. "This has been a crazy day for you, hasn't it?"

There was an understatement if she'd ever heard one, and she nodded.

The women stepped back but kept their hands on her arms. "I'm Madison, Alex's wife," the one with red hair and green eyes said.

"I'm Lauren, Court's wife," said the very pregnant blonde with spiky, pink-tipped hair.

The last one, a gorgeous blue-eyed blonde, smiled. "And I'm Taylor, Nate's wife."

They were all gorgeous, actually.

"I can't believe you're really here," Madison said. "You have no idea how hard the guys have been trying to find you."

"And instead she found us," Alex said. He glanced at his brothers. "We need to work on our investigative skills."

One of the older girls tugged on Taylor's blouse. "Is that her, Mommy?"

"Yes, sweetie, this is Kinsey, your aunt. Kinsey, this is Sarrie and next to her is her twin sister, June." She started pointing at children. "Bri, Elle, Robin, and playing on the floor with the baby is Annie. All the girls belong to Nate and me. The baby is Michael and belongs to Alex and Madison."

Nate and Taylor had six kids? Wow. "Hello, everyone." A chorus of voices answered, the older girls giving her shy smiles. Annie looked up at her and grinned, then went back to bouncing a teddy bear on Michael's stomach. Kinsey guessed the baby was about three months, and he was on his back, kicking his little feet in the air and laughing.

"Also, I'd like you to meet Rosie, my foster mother," Taylor said. "She's going to take the kids over to Court's house so we can talk without being interrupted."

A tiny woman barreled into her, wrapping her in a hug, which resulted in Rosie's face buried against her breasts. Kinsey glanced over Rosie's head, meeting Alex's amused gaze.

"She's a hugger in case you haven't noticed," he said.

When Rosie finally let go of her, she stared from Kinsey to the brothers. "You look just like your brothers, except you're a lot prettier."

"Thank you." She'd had no idea that she'd have an instant family this big, and she wasn't sure what to do with them all.

"She's overwhelmed right now," Lauren said. "Let's get the kids over to my house before she decides she doesn't want any part of this circus." She smiled at Kinsey. "You'll get used to us." She chuckled. "I hope."

While all this had been going on, Nate had stood off to the side with Court, watching. They might share the same blood, but they were two of the most intimidating men she'd ever met. Were they worried she wouldn't like their children?

"We'll help Rosie get them settled and be back in a few minutes. Don't start without us," Madison said as the women rounded up the kids.

And then Kinsey was alone with her newfound brothers and couldn't think of a thing to say. She did wonder about

Nate's six children but didn't know how to ask. He didn't strike her as a daddy kind of guy.

"You want something to drink?" Alex asked. "Wine, a beer, water, or something else?"

"No thanks." She was too nervous to drink anything.

"I'll have a beer," Nate said.

"Dude, it's your house. Get your own beer." Alex looked at her and winked.

Court chuckled. "You'll soon learn that baby brother likes poking the bear, Kinsey."

"It's the highlight of my day," Alex said. He glanced at Nate and sighed. "Fine, I'll get the beers. You sure you don't want something, Kinsey?"

She blew out a breath. "Okay, a glass of wine would be nice. Whatever you have is fine."

"I'll help," Court said. "Taylor and Madison will want a glass of wine, too." Court followed Alex to the kitchen.

Nate waved a hand at the sofa. "Come have a seat."

After she was seated, Nate parked himself in a chair, facing her. She glanced around, taking in the decor. It was homey with the comfortable brown leather furniture that was kid friendly. Toys were scattered over the floor, and a large TV was on the wall across from her. On a long table beneath the TV were game hand controls. A whole lot of them, but she supposed with all the children and adults, that was to be expected. She loved playing video games and wondered what kind they liked.

"Um, your kids are really cute."

Nate's eyes softened. "Yeah, they are. To answer the question you're dying to ask, Taylor and I adopted the girls."

"Oh, I was wondering. That's awesome." It really was, not to mention a surprise. She was fast reevaluating the assumptions she'd made about her brothers. "I have to say that the last thing I expected was to find out my brothers were FBI."

He smiled, and she guessed that he didn't do it often,

but he should. Smiling changed his entire demeanor, made him more approachable.

Court and Alex returned, each carrying a combination of wineglasses and beer bottles, which they placed on the coffee table. The wives walked in a few minutes later.

Taylor picked up a glass of wine, then perched on the arm of Nate's chair. Madison settled in next to Kinsey, with Alex on her other side. Court helped Lauren sit in another chair, and then he sat on the floor at one side of her legs, resting his arm over her knees.

When Kinsey picked up one of the wineglasses, Alex leaned across Madison and tapped his bottle against her glass. "Welcome to the family, little sister."

"Thanks." Did you hear that, Mom? I have a family again.

"I'm dying to know how you found out you have brothers," Madison said.

"It was a shock, believe me. After Mom died… our mother—"

"She's dead?" Alex said, his voice cracking.

"Yes, a little over a year ago, when I was in college. A heart attack. No warning." Her voice trembled, too.

Alex stood and walked out of the room, and she realized that this was the first time they were hearing that their mother had died. Madison hurried after Alex, and Kinsey glanced from Court to Nate. Lauren had put her hands over Court's arm, and Taylor had her head on Nate's shoulder.

There was pain in both men's eyes, and although she was sorry for putting it there, she liked them all the more for mourning a mother they hadn't seen in years, one who'd walked away from them. All the times she'd read the letter, she'd never once thought of how her mother had hurt her sons for leaving.

"I just needed a minute," Alex said, walking back into the room with his arm around Madison's shoulder.

"I'm sorry. I didn't even think about you all not knowing she was gone."

"We knew it was a possibility, but we were hoping to find both of you," Nate said, his gaze—full of love and concern—on Alex.

She cleared her throat. "I have to say it was really weird finding out that she had a life I never knew about. That I had brothers." She told them about finding the letter in her mother's Bible. "I thought you would like to read it, so I brought it with me."

She retrieved the letter from her purse. When Nate held out his hand, she gave it to him. He studied both sides of the envelope, then lifted his eyes to hers. "You've read this often."

"I have."

He handed the letter to Taylor. "Read it out loud so we can all hear it."

Kinsey leaned her head back against the sofa and closed her eyes as she listened to Taylor's voice reading the letter she knew by heart. When Taylor reached the final words of the letter, Kinsey opened her eyes, unable to stop the tears from rolling down her cheeks. As she looked around at the people in the room, she saw that everyone had tears streaming from their eyes except for Nate and Court, who both had their eyes closed tight. What were they thinking?

"'If you should decide to find your brothers, please tell them why I left. Tell them that I never stopped loving them. I only ask one thing of you, Kinsey. Be happy. I love you through eternity. Mom,'" Taylor said, then gently folded the letter and handed it back to her.

"Wow, that's so sad," Madison said.

Lauren brushed her fingers across her cheeks. "But in a way not. She saved Kinsey's life. And she was right. Her sons grew up to be amazing men." Her gaze slid over the brothers. "I don't think you guys would disagree that she laid the groundwork for who you are today."

"We searched all over Gainesville for the two of you,"

Court said.

"Why Gainesville? We lived in Jacksonville."

Nate leaned forward, resting his elbows on his knees. "Because that was the only clue we had. The man she referred to in her letter who helped her get away, she sent him a baby picture of you and the envelope was post-marked in Gainesville."

"Then she either made a brief stop there before moving on to Jacksonville, or she simply mailed it from there so no one could trace her to Jacksonville, I guess." There was so much her mother hadn't told her, and Kinsey resented that a little. "Was your father... I'm sorry, I can't even think of him as mine. Was he as awful as she said?"

"Worse," Alex said. He stood, pulled off his shirt, then turned his back to her.

Kinsey gasped at seeing the scars on his back.

"Put your damn shirt back on," Nate growled. "She doesn't need to know about him."

Alex eyed his brother as he slipped on his shirt. "Yes, she does. It's the only way she'll understand why our mother felt she had no choice but to leave. You know as well as I do, even better probably, that Mama's options were limited to either doing what she did or staying with us and risking her baby. I for one don't blame her."

"I don't either," Court softly said. "Not anymore."

Nate glanced at Taylor, and when she smiled at him, the hard lines around his mouth and eyes relaxed. Kinsey sensed that his wife was one of the few people who could calm him. She'd been subtly watching her brothers, and from the exchanged glances and touches, it was obvious all three were in love. She was both happy for them and envious.

They talked for hours, her brothers telling her about their lives and she about hers. The more time she spent with them and the more she learned about them, the more she liked them. She especially liked their wives.

When she started yawning, she said, "I think I'm going to call it a night." Her brain was on overload and needed time to digest all she'd learned. She wondered how long it would take the idea of having an instant family to settle in.

Nate pulled his phone out. "Before you leave, what's your phone number?"

Everyone grabbed their phones, and they all insisted that she put each of their numbers in hers. She left with six new family phone numbers and a promise to come over Saturday afternoon for a cookout. She'd also learned enough about her brothers not to be surprised when Alex followed her home to make sure she arrived safely.

She waved to him before entering her apartment, locking the door behind her. After kicking off her heels, she padded to the kitchen to get a glass of water. A chill snaked down her spine when she noticed her back door wasn't closed tight. She always locked it behind her when she came in from the patio. Maybe she'd been careless this morning, but she could almost visualize herself testing the doorknob to make sure it was locked. She set the glass on the counter, backed out of the room, grabbed her purse, and then ran to her car.

Was she panicking over nothing? Probably. But she wasn't one of those too-stupid-to-live women who crept through a dark house to see if an ax murderer lurked in the closet, just waiting to chop her into little pieces.

CHAPTER EIGHT

ALL RAND WANTED WAS A hot shower and his bed. These bar hours were a bitch. He'd never been a night owl, preferring to be asleep no later than midnight and up with the sun. Quiet mornings were his favorite time of day. Hopefully Nate would find a replacement for him soon. He checked his watch, sighing when he saw it would be another two hours before they could close up. At least it had been a quiet night.

His phone buzzed, his heart rate kicking up a notch at seeing Kinsey's name on the screen.

"Hold on a minute," he said, heading for the office where it was quiet. He closed the door behind him. "Hey. How was your visit with your brothers?"

"I think someone might have been in my apartment."

His body stiffened, going on full alert. "Get out. Now, Kinsey."

"I did. I'm at an all-night convenience store a few blocks from my place."

At least she was smart. "You need to call your brothers."

"If I do that, it will be like an invasion of a SEAL team or something descending on me. It's possible I didn't close my back door and lock it, but I don't think my brothers know the meaning of restraint. If they even get the hint that something might be amiss, they'll move me lock, stock, and barrel right into their compound before I can blink twice. They've already mentioned what a great idea that would be."

That didn't surprise him. "Are you inside the store?"

"Yeah."

"Stay right where you are. I'll be there in twenty." After getting the store's address from her, he went to find Josh, to let his partner know he had to leave.

★★★

The minute Rand walked into the store, she launched herself at him. "You're here."

He laughed. "That seems pretty obvious." He tucked her under his arm and led her away from the clerk's curious eyes. "You're barefoot."

"That seems pretty obvious," she said, throwing his words back at him. She lifted a foot—that was damn sexy with the cherry-red toenails—for his inspection. "I didn't take the time to grab my shoes."

"Did you notice anything else off besides your back door?"

"No. I'm probably just being silly, but I always make sure my doors and windows are locked before I leave for work. Maybe I slipped up this morning. I don't know. I'm feeling stupid now for panicking."

"No, you did the right thing. I'll follow you back to your apartment and check it out."

"Eww," she said as he walked her to her car. "I just stepped on gum."

He slipped his arms under her back and legs, picking her up.

"Eeek," she shrieked on a laugh. "You should warn a girl when you decide to go caveman on her."

He looked into her eyes and wondered if she might be the one woman he'd be willing to risk everything for. *She'll want babies.* The voice in his head brought him back to his senses. He could not, would not go there again. Not even for her.

"I'll follow you to your apartment and check it out," he said, opening her car door with his fingers and then lowering her onto the driver's seat.

When they arrived at her place, he followed her inside while keeping firm control of his hand. The one that wanted to press its palm against her back. Or curl its fingers around the back of her neck. Hell, he'd be good with touching any part of her.

"Stay right here," he said as soon as they were inside. He first eased down the hall to her bedroom, and holding his gun down by his side, he checked her closet and bathroom. Once he'd cleared those rooms, he returned to the living room, pleased to see that Kinsey hadn't moved.

"Nothing?"

"No one's here. You need to take a look, see if anything is out of place." While she did that, he went to her back door, still cracked open, and checked it over, but couldn't find any scratches in the wood that looked like someone had pried it open.

"Everything seems fine," she said, coming back to the kitchen. "I'm sorry."

Rand glanced over at her. "For what?"

"Making you come over for no reason."

"Never be sorry for staying safe, Kinsey." It probably was a matter of her not closing and locking the door, but on the outside chance someone had been in her apartment, he didn't want her staying by herself tonight. "You need a deadbolt and chain on this door." Even an amateur thief could get in without half trying.

"I've always felt safe here before tonight. First thing tomorrow I'll call the building manager and ask that he install those."

"No, I'll do it." Not all building managers could be trusted. Only two months ago the cops had arrested one for snooping in the apartments of the single female residents.

"You've already done—"

"It's not negotiable. Since I don't want you here by yourself until I make your doors secure, I'll sleep on the couch." The relief crossing her face told him that she'd been nervous about being alone.

"You don't have—"

"Also not negotiable."

She wrinkled her nose. "Turns out you're as bossy as my brothers."

"I'll take that as a compliment."

"You shouldn't," she muttered, making him grin. She glanced down, frowning at her feet. "I need a shower. My yucky feet are creeping me out."

"I'll be right here. Take your time." As he watched her walk away, he decided he was a fan of pencil skirts. The woman had curves in all the right places. He shook his head to clear it of thinking of her that way. If he dared to go there, her brothers would dump him in the Everglades for the alligators to snack on.

His stomach rumbled, reminding him that the last food in his belly had been Helena's cookies. While Kinsey was showering, he rummaged around in her kitchen. By the time she came out, he had a pot of coffee brewing and a plate of cheese, crackers, and grapes.

"Well look at you, all domesticated. A man who knows his way around a kitchen is a real turn-on for a girl, you know."

He glanced over his shoulder, the smart comeback dying on his lips. Her feet were bare, her hair was down around her shoulders, and her black boxer shorts and red camisole were sexy as hell. He swallowed hard. She's off-limits, his brain said. His dick disagreed.

"You want a cup of coffee?"

The light in her eyes faded when he didn't flirt back. "No, I'd be up all night." She came next to him, brushing against his arm as she reached for a glass filled with water sitting on the counter.

She was killing him. He picked up the plate and his coffee, then moved to her pub table. "So how did it go with your brothers tonight?"

"Really good." She added a few ice cubes to her water, then came to the table. "I don't think it's sunk in yet that they're my brothers, though. I mean, for all my life, it was just me and Mom. And then all of a sudden I have three brothers, three sisters-in-law, and a horde of adorable nieces and nephews. It's overwhelming."

"They're good people, Kinsey." He put a slice of cheese on a cracker, then handed it to her.

"I'm seeing that. My sisters-in-laws are pretty awesome. I'm going to have to stand my ground with my brothers, I'm thinking. They're already trying to boss me around."

That wasn't a surprise. "How so?"

"For one thing, thinking I should move into their compound." She narrowed her eyes. "Stop laughing. It's not funny."

"It kind of is." He wondered if his name had come up in conversation. "They'll want to vet all your dates."

She groaned. "Oh joy." When he laughed again, she lifted mischief-filled eyes to his. He was sure whatever she was thinking spelled trouble. "Since I'm positive they've already vetted you, you can be my date for Saturday."

"What's happening on Saturday?"

"A"—she made air quotes—"family cookout. It's in the afternoon, so you'll be able to get to Aces and Eights when you need to."

Yep. Trouble with a capital T. "That's not a good idea, Kinsey. Your brothers aren't going to want me anywhere near you."

"Why? You're a good man. If you don't meet with their approval, then no one will."

"It's a bro code thing." It sounded silly saying it out loud. There was more to it than that, though. Her brothers knew he had issues, and they'd want better for her. A man who would put a ring on her finger and give her a family.

"A bro code? Seriously, Rand? That's high-school shit. It's…" She threw up her hands. "It's stupid." She sat back and put her foot on the edge of his chair. "It's just a date, not a marriage proposal. Besides, my brothers aren't the boss of me, no matter what they might think."

He grinned. She didn't have a clue how strong-willed the Gentrys were, but he'd leave her with her illusions for now. She poked his thigh with her toes, and he glanced down. Even her feet were sexy. "Is that a tat?" He picked up her foot for a closer look, realizing his mistake when he touched her. Her skin was soft, her toenails painted cherry red, and the sole was pale pink.

"It's a hummingbird." She leaned over and studied the tattoo just above her ankle. "My mother loved them. I got it shortly after she died."

"That makes it special along with being very pretty."

"Thanks. So, about Saturday. I'm all the more determined to show up with you as my date. My brothers need to know that they can't decide my life for me."

He absolutely should say no but found it impossible to refuse her. "You do realize I'm risking life and limb by agreeing, right?"

She laughed. "My hero."

"I don't know about that. I'll be walking into the lion's den, so more like too stupid to live." He loved the way she laughed—deep from her throat and carefree, her eyes sparkling with amusement. He'd grown up in a world where emotions were checked at the door. One didn't laugh too hard or too long, and you didn't wear your heart on your sleeve for all to see. Maybe that was why he found Kinsey so refreshing. She was honest and open, not to mention mouthwateringly sexy. He had the feeling that when she did fall in love, that she would love hard. He wished he could be that man.

"It's getting late," she said on a yawn.

When she looked at him with a question in her eyes, he

smiled with true regret. "You got a spare pillow?"

The light faded from her eyes. "Right. The stupid bro code. You're bigger, so you take my bed."

"Odds are you accidently left your door cracked, but on the off chance you didn't and whoever it was decides to return, my gun and I'll be waiting on the couch."

She shrugged. "Whatever."

After she'd tossed a pillow and blanket to him, then disappeared into her room without a word, Rand checked to make sure all the windows and doors were secure. Then he spent a restless night on a too-short, uncomfortable sofa wondering exactly why he wasn't wrapped around Kinsey in her bed.

♣

Kinsey blinked sleepy eyes, trying to focus on the e-mail that had popped up in her in-box from Summer Fashions' owner. Having the sexiest man she'd ever known sleeping one room away from her hadn't made for a restful night. She'd heard of the bro code, but she'd thought it was only a thing in romance novels meant to keep the hero and heroine apart until they realized how stupid that was. That guys actually believed they had to honor such a dumb rule blew her mind. What business was it to her brothers who she dated?

"Did you get the invitation, too?" Corrie asked, coming up behind Kinsey and reading over her shoulder.

"Appears so. Is the Friends of the Library's Gala a big deal?" She scanned the invitation. She'd never been to a black-tie event and knew for a fact she didn't have a suitable outfit in her closet.

Corrie gasped. "How can you even ask that?"

"Poor college student here." Kinsey pointed at herself. "'Gala' wasn't a word in my vocabulary. I guess I can't decline since the invitation's from the big boss?"

"Not even. I buy a new dress for it each year."

Kinsey groaned, thinking of the hit her credit card was about to take. "I guess we better go shopping."

An hour later Kinsey walked out of the dressing room and stood in front of the three-way mirrors. "What do you think?"

Corrie's gaze ran over her. "I think I'd die to have your figure. It's perfect."

"Yeah?" The fitted red dress was sophisticated yet subtly sexy with the off-the-shoulder bodice that showed just enough cleavage to be daring, but not something she'd constantly be tugging up to keep her nipples covered when she wore it. She stepped away from the mirrors, then walked back, eyeing the slit that ran halfway up her thigh. With each step she took, her left leg was briefly exposed before being covered by the material again. She'd never owned a dress that made her feel this sensual, and she wished Rand could see her in it.

"Definitely perfect. All you need with the dress are these"—Corrie handed her a pair of strappy silver shoes with four-inch heels—"and these silver dangling earrings. Paint your fingernails and toenails red, and that's it. Nothing else."

Kinsey slipped on the shoes. Except for one thing, Corrie was right. Anything else would distract from the overall effect, so no rings, bracelets, or a necklace. Just the earrings and the silver hair comb her mother had given her one Christmas. The dress cost more than she'd ever spent on one, but she did get an employee discount, so that helped.

She grinned. "Sold. Ring me up."

"Well, aren't you a man's wet dream?"

"Leave her alone, Sebastian," Corrie said before walking away.

"Why should I?" he said, stepping into Kinsey's personal space. "Not when you look like this."

Kinsey backed away from him. "You should do as Corrie says and leave me alone."

"Hasn't anyone ever told you the chase is half the fun, Kinsey? The faster you try to run…" He left the rest unsaid as he stroked his knuckles over her cheek.

She slapped his hand away. "Go find someone else to bother, Sebastian."

"Can't. You're just too irresistible. But I'm here to tell you to mark your calendar for a week from Friday."

"I know. I got the invitation this morning."

"Good. Wear that dress. Red looks hot on you."

Her eyes narrowed on his retreating back. *Or what? You'll fire me?* He'd bothered her a little when she'd only been part-time—mostly by making stupid suggestive remarks—but it had gotten worse in the last few months. Did he think just because she was now full-time that she was fair game? She hadn't done anything to encourage him, had stayed out of his way as much as possible, and she didn't know why he was focusing his attentions on her.

As much as she loved her job, it was time to find another one. It burned, though, that she'd have to walk away from a position she loved because of one jerk of a man. Her only other option was to file a sexual harassment suit, but the business was family owned and if she went that route, they'd make her life miserable.

She headed to the dressing room to change back into her clothes. No way was she going to wear the red dress now. The store also had the same one in black, and she bought that one instead.

Back at her desk, she called Aiden. She needed a drink night with her friend. She got his voice mail. Since he'd been drafted by the Dolphins, she hadn't seen much of him, and she was missing her friend. He didn't even know she'd met her brothers. After leaving a message to call her, she made a cup of coffee, then settled down and got busy.

Later that morning Kinsey was at her computer, working on a purchase order for one of her vendors. Her phone's intercom buzzed.

She punched the button. "Kinsey here."

"You have some visitors," Shannon, one of the sales associates, said, sounding breathless.

Some? "Did you get their names?"

"No, but they said they're your brothers. Oh my God, Kinsey, how did I not know you had three brothers who looked like this? I'm going to hang up now and go stare at them and drool." The line went dead.

What were her brothers doing here? She touched up her lipstick and then headed to the sales floor. Sure enough, there they were. And there was Shannon and Carly leaning on the register counter, both girls with dreamy looks on their faces as they watched the guys roam around the store.

Kinsey shook her head and grinned. She supposed she couldn't blame the two. The Gentry brothers were definitely easy on the eyes. Coming up behind Shannon and Carly, she said, "Boo." Both girls jumped.

"Introduce us," Shannon demanded.

"Did you not check out their hands? All three are wearing wedding rings."

"I don't care," Carly said and then giggled.

Shannon nodded. "What she said."

After giving them an eye roll, Kinsey went to greet her brothers. "Hey, guys, this is a surprise."

"You're my prettiest sister," Alex said as he hugged her.

She scoffed. "Easy for you to say since I'm your only one." She was learning that her youngest brother was a hugger.

"Stop hogging her, baby brother." Court pulled her away from Alex, giving her a brief hug.

"You can't call me that anymore, dude. She's the baby of the family now," Alex said.

Court smirked. "Don't hold your breath, *dude.*"

From Nate she got a shoulder squeeze. She'd take it. "So what's up?"

"We came to take you to lunch," Court said.

"Cool. Let me grab my purse." As she passed Shannon and Carly, still staring at her brothers, she said, "You both are about to embarrass yourselves by drooling." Smiling, she got her purse and then walked with her brothers across the street to an Italian bistro.

After they ordered, Alex asked if she liked her job.

"I love it. I have a good eye for what sells, and that's not something you can really teach. It would be perfect if the owner's son would keep his hands to himself." As soon as the words were out of her mouth, she knew she shouldn't have let that slip. Three pairs of eyes went stone-cold, giving her a glimpse of how dangerous these men could be.

"But I can handle him," she hurried to add.

"You shouldn't have to." Nate exchanged some kind of silent message with his brothers, then said, "What's his name?"

"None of your business." The last thing she needed was three FBI agents meddling in her life. Even so, warmth spread through her that they wanted to protect her. She wasn't alone anymore.

Alex snorted. "Nice try, little sister. It will take us less than ten minutes to get a name."

She met Nate's gaze straight on. "I'm sure he's right, but don't. It's my life and my problem to deal with." For good measure she shifted her gaze to Court and Alex to include them.

"On one condition," Nate said. "The day it goes beyond what you can handle, you tell one of us."

Court nodded. "The thing you have to remember, Kinsey, is men like that don't take no for an answer. Better you tell us when it starts making you uneasy than to let it go too far and we have to kill him."

She choked on the water she was swallowing. "You're kidding, right?" Of course they were. They were federal agents and couldn't just go around killing people. Could they?

"Probably," Alex said, grinning at her.

Although Nate wasn't smiling, there was amusement in his eyes, and she realized they were messing with her. She was going to have to get used to their odd sense of humor. How did they see her? Was she more or less than what they'd expected or hoped for? She wasn't comfortable enough to ask, but she realized that it did matter. She wanted them to like her.

There was something else she wanted to know that had been on her mind since she'd met them. She'd wanted to ask last night but decided it might be an uncomfortable discussion to have in front of their wives. They might not like the question, but she needed to know. She hesitated, though, not sure how to ask.

"If there's something you want to know, just ask," Nate said.

She blinked. Was she that easy to read?

Alex chuckled. "He's omniscient. You might as well get used to it."

"Now that's scary." She didn't like to think anyone could read her mind.

"Tell me about it," Alex said. "He spoiled all my fun growing up. He knew the mischief I was about to get into before I did."

Nate smirked. "Still do."

"Truth." Alex glanced at her. "Back to what you want to ask but are afraid to."

The waiter arrived with their lunch, giving her time to get her thoughts together. Her brothers were sharing an extra-large pizza that smelled delicious. She took a bite of her Greek salad, trying to ignore the tantalizing aroma of cheese and pepperoni.

Without asking, Nate put a slice onto a plate and slid it over to her. "You know you want it."

She narrowed her eyes at him. "Get out of my head, big brother." Both Court and Alex laughed, and she grinned at them. "Is that how to handle him? Just dig my feet in and don't let him steamroll right over me?"

"Good luck with that," Court said. "It never worked for us." He glanced at Alex, getting a nod. "But quit stalling, little sister. What's on your mind?"

She really liked how they kept calling her their sister. Yes, she did have a question, and what did she have to lose? She'd already figured out if they didn't want to answer, they wouldn't. "I get that you didn't know about me until recently, but why didn't you try to find my mother... our mother once you were adults?"

All three of her brothers sat back in their chairs while Court and Alex looked to Nate to answer. Was it that hard of a question?

Nate dropped the last half of his slice of pizza onto his plate as if her question had destroyed his appetite. He looked sad—they all did—and she wished she could snatch her question back. "I'm sorry. You don't have to answer."

"You deserve to know," Nate said. He met her gaze straight on. "I'm not making excuses, but we were just boys, conditioned by our father not to question anything he said. We each had a part of the puzzle of why our mother left us, but to protect each other from what we *assumed* was the truth, we didn't share what we knew until recently. That is my one regret. If we had, we would have realized much sooner that she had a precious life to protect. You." He dropped his napkin on the table. "I need to get back to the office for a meeting." He looked at Court and then Alex. "Make sure she gets safely back to work."

Confused, Kinsey watched him walk away.

"He'll never forgive himself for believing the worst of our mother," Alex softly said. "We all should have known better."

Court pushed his plate away. "Alex was too young to understand anything, so the blame mostly goes to Nate and me. I thought she was pregnant with another man's baby because of a fight I overheard. Our bastard of a father accused her of being a whore. He beat her in an attempt to make her miscarry. At first she denied his accusations, but then in an effort to get him to stop, she admitted he wasn't the father. It wasn't until recently that I understood she was only telling him what he wanted to hear."

She was that baby, yet it seemed as if they were talking about someone else. Their childhoods hadn't been close to the wonderful life she'd had with her mother. "How old were you when that happened?"

"Nine."

She reached across the table and put her hand on his. "A child shouldn't have to witness a scene like that, much less understand it for what it was." She was beginning to get why her mother hadn't revealed her secrets. The memories of being married to a man capable of that kind of violence would have been ones she'd do her best to forget.

Court gave her the ghost of a smile. "I know, but I still should have known better."

"He didn't tell Nate or me about witnessing that fight when it happened," Alex said. "Then when she walked away, Nate followed her to the highway. A man who'd worked for our old man doing odd jobs picked her up. Nate thought she was leaving us for him, and he kept that to himself because he didn't want us to think the worst of her. Once all of this came out, Nate tracked the man down and found out all he'd done was drive her to the bus station."

"Please don't cry," Alex said when she swiped at the tears rolling down her cheeks. "From what you've told us, she was happy in her life with you. We don't blame her for leaving."

"The tears aren't for her. She was happy and had a good life. My heart hurts for the three of you, being left with someone that cruel."

Court shook his head. "She did what she had to do to

save you. We wouldn't change a thing about that."

That was the moment her heart filled with uncondi-tional love for her brothers.

CHAPTER NINE

R AND STOPPED BY SUMMER FASHIONS to give
Kinsey the keys to her new locks.

"Well, hello. I'm Shannon. How may I help you?"

He smiled at the pretty blonde-haired woman whose
eyes were blatantly roaming over him. "Is Kinsey Landon
available?"

Her lips formed a pout. "It's so not fair."

"Pardon?"

"Kinsey's getting all the hot guys today. She needs to
share, dontcha think?"

"Um, I guess that's up to her." What hot guys were visiting Kinsey?

"Are you one of her brothers, too? And please don't tell
me you're also married."

"No, just a friend. Is she around?" He thought it best
to ignore her second question. It wasn't good that he was
relieved Kinsey's visitors were her brothers. He'd spent
the morning convincing himself that he was going to step
away. But that streak of jealousy that had heated his blood
when thinking Kinsey had hot-guy visitors said putting
distance between them might be harder than he thought.

"No. She went to lunch with her brothers, but she should
be back in about ten minutes if you want to wait. You can
keep me company." Shannon peered up at him with bright
eyes and a hopeful smile.

This one was a man-eater, so definitely not a good idea.
And it positively wouldn't be wise to be here if her broth-

ers came back with her. "Do you have an envelope you can give me?" Although leaving the keys with Shannon probably wasn't a good idea. She didn't strike him as being a responsible kind of girl.

"For you? Sure."

He followed her to the cash stand, then managed not to roll his eyes when she pulled an envelope from a drawer and wrote a phone number on it.

"Here you go," she said, holding the envelope so that her number was impossible to miss. "I don't usually give out my number before I know a guy's name." She giggled. "For you I'm making an exception. What is your name, anyway?"

An older woman walked out from the back, saving him from having to answer. She glanced from him to Shannon to the envelope that Shannon tried to crush into his hand when the woman appeared. Not wanting to get the girl in trouble, he took it and stuffed it into his pant pocket. A bell dinged as three women walked in.

"Shannon, please go help those ladies," the woman said.

"Oh, all right." She winked at him before bouncing away.

Rand seriously considered kissing the woman for saving him from Shannon's clutches.

"I know. You're about to thank me for rescuing you." The woman chuckled. "Shannon's a great sales associate unless you're what she calls a hot guy; then she goes a little crazy. I'm Corrie, Kinsey's boss. Can I help you?"

"Actually, you can." He pulled the envelope from his pocket. "Would you make sure this goes straight to Kinsey?" At her nod he lifted a pen from a cup on the counter, crossed out Shannon's phone number, and after writing Kinsey's name on the envelope, he dropped the two sets of keys in it and then sealed it.

Back at his car, he texted Kinsey, letting her know that her boss had her new keys. Before he could pull out of the parking space, he spied her crossing the street, flanked by Alex and Court. He couldn't quite figure out what it was about her that drew him. He'd never felt an instant connection with any other woman the way he had Kinsey, not even with his ex-wife. It wasn't just that she was beautiful with a killer body, although he appreciated both those things.

He waited until they disappeared into the store before driving away. As much as he wanted to explore this thing between them, there were some good reasons not to. His own issues being a big one, not to mention three overgrown and overprotective brothers with the ability to put a serious hurt on him if he was ever the reason for so much as one tiny tear leaked out of their sister's eye. And yet he couldn't seem to stay away from her.

☾

Saturday afternoon Rand pushed the intercom button at the Gentrys' gate. He glanced over at Kinsey. "Did you tell them I was coming with you?"

She grinned. "Nope. I thought it would be a fun surprise."

"Not so sure about that. Maybe I should have worn my bulletproof vest."

"I won't let them shoot you." She leaned over the console and waved her fingers at the gate's camera. "I promised him you won't kill him. Let us in."

"You shouldn't make promises you can't keep, little sister." The gate swung open.

Rand snorted as he looked at Kinsey. "Told you." That had been Nate, and there had not been amusement in his voice.

"He can sure sound scary when he wants to," she said, dramatically widening her eyes, making him chuckle.

"You're not intimidated by them?"

"I was at first, but we've had a few really good talks. For all their gruff, they're marshmallows inside."

"Uh-huh." There was that throaty laugh that he loved. When he brought the car to a stop in front of Nate's house, all three brothers were standing on the porch, their arms crossed over their chest. "Remember. You promised to protect me."

"Come on, scaredy cat. Let's go see the big bad wolves."

He followed her up the sidewalk, and damn did she look hot. She had on a white denim skirt, a red sleeveless blouse, and red and black cowboy boots.

"Stevens," Nate said.

So he was Stevens again. He nodded.

"Stop staring at him with those death glares, boys." Kinsey gave each of her brothers a hug, then took his hand. "Let's go say hi to their wives. They're a lot nicer."

Nate's gaze narrowed at their joined hands. "You can come in, Kinsey. He can't."

"Bro, stop being a jerk," Alex said, using his body to push Nate away. He smiled at his sister. "He can come in if you want him to. If not, his ass is grass." He winked at her.

"I prefer his ass the way it is now, thank you very much."

Alex snorted. "You're going to be good training for when his girls start bringing boys home."

"There will be no boys coming through that gate," Nate growled.

"Oh, jeez, your poor daughters," Kinsey said, rolling her eyes. "Or with six of them, maybe poor you."

Rand agreed with both scenarios but wisely kept his mouth shut.

"Everyone's out back." Court opened the door, then stepped back to let Kinsey enter.

"A minute, Stevens," Nate said, putting his hand on Rand's shoulder.

And here it was, his warning.

Kinsey squeezed his hand. "If you let him send you packing, I'll lose all respect for you."

He dipped his chin, grinning at her. "I'll do my best to

make sure you still respect me in the morning. Not making any promises, though. He's scary."

"Been nice knowing you," Alex said a bit too cheerfully. He pulled Kinsey into the house. Court followed them in, closing the door behind him.

"She's not for you," Nate said, getting right down to business.

Rand jammed his hands into his pockets. "She might think differently."

"Listen, it's not that you're not good enough for her." Nate huffed out a breath. "You're one of the best, and I wouldn't worry that you'd treat her wrong. But your head's not in the right place now for a relationship with any woman, especially my sister."

"Are you ordering me away from her?" He didn't know why he didn't make his boss happy and just walk away from Kinsey. He'd told himself a hundred times he was going to do exactly that. But for the first time since losing his daughter, he was living again. Kinsey made him happy. Was it fair to give that up without talking to her? If she understood where he was coming from and agreed that they could enjoy each other's company without any expectations, then what was the harm?

"As much as I want to, no. She's still learning what it's like to have brothers—"

"And overprotective ones at that."

Nate cracked a rare smile. "There is that. I'm already seeing she can be stubborn—"

"Wonder where she got that from?"

"Would you shut up a minute? What I'm trying to say—"

"Is that who I see is none of your business," Kinsey said from behind him.

Rand glanced over his shoulder to see Kinsey leaning in the doorway. Christ, she was as stealthy as her brothers.

She slipped her arm through Nate's. "Now leave him alone and come inside. And both of you play nice."

As she led her brother away, she glanced over her shoulder and winked. Rand smirked at Nate's retreating back. The man was already wrapped around his sister's little finger and was clueless. He followed them to the backyard, missing a step when he saw all the Gentry children. How had he not thought about them being here? He avoided children. It hurt too much to hear their laughter, to look into their bright eyes and know he'd never again see his daughter's blue ones, or to be graced with one of her sweet smiles.

His heart jumped into a panic beat—as if it was too broken to stay in his chest—the way it had started doing every time he saw a child after Zoe died. He turned to leave, needing to get out of here before he lost his shit in front of everyone.

"Hey. You okay?" Kinsey said, coming up next to him and slipping her arm around his. "You're trembling."

"I have to go."

A giggling shriek filled the air, startling him. He swung his gaze toward the sound to see Annie on her back, her little legs kicking as Alex tickled her. Zoe loved it... *had* loved it when he tickled her.

"More, Daddy," she'd cry when he stopped.

"I have to go," he said again, hating the desperation he heard in his voice. He turned back in time to see understanding settle in Kinsey's eyes as she looked from Annie to him. She slid her hand down to his, tangling their fingers. The touch of her palm against his, her warmth seeping into his skin, was so soothing that he fought the urge to drag her out with him. All he wanted to do was take her home and lose himself in her body until the only thing in his head was her.

"You can go if you need to, but maybe it's time to learn how to be around children. If it helps, I won't leave your side."

He tightened his hand around hers. "Your brother's right.

I'm not good for you right now." So why wasn't he letting go of her?

Kinsey held tight to Rand's hand when he tried to pull away. "My brother needs to mind his own business." She glanced over to the patio where Court was putting hamburgers and hot dogs on the grill. "Come with me."

Clutching her hand as if she were his lifeline, he let her take him to Court. She'd seen the pain in his eyes when he'd looked at Annie, and her heart hurt for him. Even missing her mother with a bone-deep ache, she knew it couldn't possibly compare to losing a child. Maybe she should have let him leave, but he couldn't hide from children forever. Well, she supposed he could, but what kind of life was that?

As they passed the cooler, she stopped long enough to grab a beer and a water. When they reached Court, she said, "Go away. We're taking over."

"What? You afraid I'll put a laxative or something in his?"

"Yep. So bye." He'd said it with a smirk, but she'd caught the concern in his eyes when he'd glanced at Rand. She'd already noticed that her brothers were observant, and she supposed they were trained to notice even the small things.

"I'm sorry," Rand said after Court joined the others.

"For?" She handed him both bottles. "Open the beer for me, will you?"

His gaze dropped to the bottles he held, and she saw shame on his face, saw the unshed tears in his eyes. He was embarrassed that he'd almost lost it in front of her. She hated that he felt like he had to hide his love for his daughter from her, from anyone. It didn't make him weak. It made him a beautiful man who'd loved a little girl and didn't know how to come back from losing her.

"For ruining your day. Sometimes…" He twisted off the bottle cap with his fingers.

She put her hand on his arm. "I know. A few days ago a woman came into the store wearing a blouse just like my mother's. It was her favorite one. I had to leave the sales floor before I lost it." She took the opened beer from him. "There will always be times when something reminds you of her, especially other children. Don't feel embarrassed because you loved her so much it hurts. She was a lucky little girl to have you as her daddy."

"I was the lucky one," he murmured. He picked up the spatula and flipped over the burgers.

"Without a doubt." She smiled at the sight of her brothers on their backs on the grass as Nate's daughters climbed over them. "From what I understand, Nate and Taylor's girls had a rough start in life. All the children in the world should have daddies like you or my brothers."

As she'd hoped, his gaze shifted to the laughing children. He watched them for a few seconds, and the ghost of a smile appeared on his face before he looked away. He didn't seem to be trembling the way he had at seeing them earlier.

She wasn't a doctor, but she thought he might be suffering from something similar to PTSD and should probably talk to a professional. She thought it would be good for him to try to acclimate to being around children again, and maybe she could help with that.

"Thank you," he said, lifting beautiful blue eyes that were a little brighter to hers.

Not wanting to put too much emphasis on his reaction to the kids, before or now when he'd almost smiled, and in an attempt to lighten the mood, she tapped a finger on her lips. "You can show your appreciation by kissing me."

His gaze fell to said lips. "Your brothers are probably going to shoot me right where I stand for this, but I don't care."

He lowered his face, and the moment their mouths touched, she vaguely wondered when her knees had turned to limp noodles. She moaned when his tongue skimmed over the seam of her lips. He answered with a groan that she felt in places no other man had touched.

"Get your mouth off my sister."

They jerked apart, and she glared at her youngest brother. He winked, letting her know he was messing with them. Ignoring Alex, Rand turned his attention to the meat on the grill.

"Dude, you know what you're doing? Have you ever even had a hot dog?" Alex said.

Rand tilted his head as he stared down at the hot dogs on the grill. "Once, when the chef was sick." He smirked at Alex. "Mother boiled some."

Her brother stared at him in horror. "She boiled them?" At Rand's nod Alex put his hand on her arm, giving her a push. "Go visit the others. I have some serious grilling lessons to give this boy."

She lifted her brows, silently asking Rand if he was going to be okay, getting a smile and a nod. Trusting that Alex would play nice, she joined her sisters-in-law. "Sorry I didn't come say hi right away." She settled in one of the lawn chairs.

Taylor glanced over at Rand. "You were where you needed to be. I was surprised to see him here. We've invited him over several times since he lost Zoe, but he always refused. It's hard for him to be around children."

"Understandable," Lauren said, rubbing her belly as if soothing the baby nesting inside. "I don't know if I could be if something happened to mine."

Madison kissed the forehead of the baby sleeping on her shoulder. "It slayed me when my father was killed, but I think I'd lay down and die if something happened to Michael."

"I think you're good for him, Kinsey," Taylor said, her gaze alighting on Rand. "That you were able to get him here speaks volumes."

They watched as Nate ambled over to the grill. Kinsey rolled her eyes when he bumped his shoulder against

Rand, sending Rand sideways. "They need to stop picking on him."

Lauren grinned. "He can take it." She turned curious eyes to Kinsey. "So, you and Rand, huh? How'd that happen?"

"I don't know if there is a me and Rand, but I really like him. He seems to think that he's not in a good enough place right now to have a relationship. That it wouldn't be fair to me." Nate strolled over, and she narrowed her eyes at him. "Big brother isn't helping by going all macho and warning Rand away."

The Gentry wives all laughed. "Insider info here," Taylor said, still chuckling. "Your brothers are the equivalent of mama bears and tend to get overzealous in doing their job of safeguarding those under their protection. That now includes you."

Nate nodded. "Damn straight."

"I wasn't finished, babe. What I was going to say before being interrupted, take their protection when it's needed, but ignore them when they try to tell you what's best for you."

When Nate growled at that, Kinsey couldn't help her laugh. "Good advice."

"Now go away, husband. We're having girl talk here." Her gaze roamed appreciatively over Nate. "And you're obviously not a girl."

"Thank God," he said with a dramatic shudder. "I was sent to tell you that the burgers are done."

Taylor stood and put her hand on Lauren's shoulder. "You go sit. Madison, put your son in his crib, then help Court round up the girls. Kinsey, go make sure Rand doesn't sneak out on us. Nate, you can come help me with the potato salad and stuff."

"She's a bossy girl," Nate said, shooting Kinsey a wink.

"I don't think he minds at all," Kinsey said, watching him sling an arm around his wife as they walked away.

Madison chuckled. "I don't think there's another woman in the world he'd let boss him around, but he loves for her to. She's also the best thing that's ever happened to him. Your brother never smiled before her."

Every time she heard something like that about one of her brothers, she wanted to cry.

CHAPTER TEN

"YOU'RE A COOL DUDE, DUDE, and Nate likes you," Alex said.

Rand wasn't so sure. Nate used to like him, but put Kinsey in the mix and maybe not so much anymore. "I hear a but. And did you just say the word 'dude' twice in a row?"

Alex scrunched his eyebrows together. "Did I?" He shrugged. "Whatever. The but is, you hurt our sister and we'll make your life miserable until the day you die." Alex slapped him on the back. "Now that I got that brotherly shit out of the way, you should also know that I don't think she could have picked a better man."

"Thanks for that, but don't go sending out wedding invitations, *dude*."

"If you're talking about my wedding, *dudes*, you better include me in the discussion." Kinsey put her hand on his upper arm and smiled. "So when are we getting married?"

Ignoring Alex's snicker, he said, "I was thinking next Saturday would be a good day, Sunshine." Her smile turned brilliant, and he realized that was exactly what she'd brought into his sorry life. Sunshine. He'd lived in the dark for so long, had thought it would always be this way after losing Zoe, but here this woman was, showing him a way out. What could he offer her, though?

She tsked. "Oh no. A week isn't nearly enough time to plan a wedding and honeymoon. Let's just elope."

"Even better. I've always wanted to be married in Vegas

by an Elvis impersonator."

"There will be no eloping, little sister." Alex tapped a finger on her nose. "Your only problem's going to be choosing which brother to walk you down the aisle. Since I'm your favorite, you should pick me."

Rand smirked. "What makes you think you're her favorite?"

"Duh, dude. I'm the prettiest brother, the most fun, and I can take either one of them down without trying."

That was true. Alex had a black belt in Krav Maga. The only one of them equal to him in the art was Taylor. He glanced at Kinsey, who had the biggest grin on her face as she stared at Alex in total fascination.

He leaned over and whispered in her ear. "Alex can kill with nothing more than his pinkie. We're definitely eloping." They were joking around, but when she lifted those beautiful eyes that he kept getting lost in, he suddenly wished they weren't. This thing he had for her was happening entirely too fast.

She exhaled as if her lungs could no longer hold air. Was she feeling it too?

"Get a room," Alex muttered.

Rand tore his gaze away from Kinsey's. Before her, if anyone had asked him to describe his ideal woman, it would have been along the lines of his ex-wife. Willowy, blonde, blue-eyed, reserved. Kinsey was none of those things, but he wanted her more than he'd ever wanted another woman.

She let out an adorable giggle-snort sound. "I'm beginning to understand what a pain in the butt brothers can be."

"Hey," Alex said. "I resemble that remark."

"We're getting hungry over here," Court yelled as if cued to confirm Kinsey's opinion on brothers.

Alex picked up the platter of meat. "Let's go feed the masses."

As he turned to follow, Rand saw Nate's girls sitting at a small table set up next to the bigger one, and he stilled. How had he forgotten about them? As if sensing his hesitation, Kinsey slipped her hand into his.

"You hear the one about the man who walked into a bar with a slab of asphalt under his arm? He said, 'A beer, please, and one for the road.' You can laugh now." She looked up at him, vigorously blinking her eyes.

This woman. "Thank you," he said, squeezing her hand. He followed her to the round patio table, pulled out a chair for her, and then sat next to her. Maybe it was time to learn to be around children again. It didn't escape him that it was because of her—maybe for her—that he would even want to be figuratively opening the curtains and letting the light in.

Across from him, Alex wore a canvas carrier, holding Michael to his chest. He stuck a pacifier in his son's mouth. Baby Michael looked at Rand, spit out the pacifier, and then gave Rand a big, toothless, drooling grin. Rand made a face at him, and the boy shrieked and kicked his little legs, making Rand smile. It hurt enough to have him putting his hand on his chest, over his heart, but he didn't have the urge to get up and run away.

Progress. And it felt good. Damn good. He darted a glance at Kinsey to see a soft smile on her face as she watched him. He winked at her, letting her know he was okay. She put her hand on his leg and squeezed. His heart tripped over itself as they stared at each other.

Nate cleared his throat. "When you two are done making eyes at each other, let me know so we can eat."

"We're not—"

"Dude, you so are," Alex said.

"Du," Michael screamed, kicking his feet against Alex's stomach.

"Dear God, not him, too," Rand muttered.

Alex thought that was hilarious, which set off his son, the

two of them—carbon copies of each other—laughing like demented hyenas. Their glee seemed contagious as the rest of the Gentrys joined in, including Kinsey. Well, except for Nate, who wore a scowl as he tried to stare Rand down. But Rand saw the amusement in his eyes, and it was then he knew. The Gentry brothers might razz him over Kinsey, doing their best to give him a hard time, but—although they probably wouldn't say so—they approved. He qualified that. As long as he didn't hurt her. Then all bets were off.

"I have something to say," Kinsey said, drawing all eyes to her. "I can't tell you how awesome it's turning out to be to have brothers, to have a family. But—"

"I knew there was a but coming," Nate muttered.

"Yes, there is. You three can't just stomp your way into my life and start dictating what I can and can't do." She pointed her knife at Nate. "Especially you."

"She's got your number," Taylor said, smirking at her husband.

Court chuckled. "You're too smart for your own good, little sister."

"Dude," Alex said. "What do you expect? She's got our genes. Of course she's smart."

She grinned at Alex. "Being a Gentry makes me smart?"

"Well, duh."

"Oh, oh, oh," Madison said, bouncing in her seat. "She's the queen of diamonds."

"I'm what?"

"When they were undercover at Aces and Eights, Alex was known as the jack of hearts, Court the king of clubs, and Nate the ace of spades," Lauren explained. "They always thought the bar was the queen of diamonds. Little did they know they had a sister, but they do, so you're the queen."

"I can do queen," Kinsey said, doing an impressive imitation of a queen wave, getting more laughter from her new family.

Rand watched the byplay between Kinsey and her brothers with amusement, immeasurably pleased that she'd found a family worthy of her, men who knew how to love and protect what was theirs. She was pretty independent and might not like the idea of being under their protection, but that was how men thought, political correctness be damned.

They needed to have a serious talk. He might be working toward being comfortable around children again, but nothing would change his mind about having another one. It was more than the fear of losing another child. If he did have one, he would be a nervous wreck, afraid to let his kid out of his sight. He'd want to keep his child away from other children and their contagious germs. He'd end up smothering the poor kid with his fears of all the things that could steal his child from him, like the fucking flu. One sneeze would have him speed-dialing an ambulance.

Before he worked himself into a knot of anxiety, he closed down his thoughts. Now wasn't the time for them, but Kinsey needed to understand where he was coming from before anything more happened between them. So they would talk, and where they went from here would be her decision.

"No, Annie. Frogs don't like hot dogs."

"Froggie hungry, Rosie," Annie said.

Rand glanced over to see the youngest of Nate and Taylor's girls trying to feed a hot dog to her stuffed frog. Zoe had had a frog, and it was something she would have done. For a brief second, the pain of missing her was intense. Then a memory of her came, the time she put her frog in the toilet because it needed a bath, and he found himself smiling.

Rosie, Taylor's foster mother and now the girls' nanny, handed Annie a carrot to feed her frog. That seemed to satisfy Annie, and peace was restored. That he smiled now when thinking of his daughter seemed a miracle.

C

"Today wasn't so bad, was it?"

Rand turned his head toward Kinsey. They were back at her apartment, sitting on her back patio. "It was good. Really good." He had a few hours before he needed to head to the bar for the night, and he'd asked for a little time to talk.

"I'm glad you stayed, but I wouldn't have thought any less of you if you hadn't."

"The truth, I wouldn't have if you hadn't been with me." He reached over and took her hand in his. "We do need to talk, though."

"Okay, I'm listening."

"I like you, Kinsey. A lot. There's something between us, and I think you feel it, too." She nodded. "But I need you to know that I'll never have another child."

"Because?"

She wasn't going to make this easy. He let go of her hand and stood. The tinkling noise of her fountain was a soothing sound, and he stared at it, trying to collect his thoughts. Did she come out here often to read a book, or maybe to just sit and think? There were so many things he wanted to know about her, but wasn't he being selfish to want to see her when, in the end, there was nothing he could promise her?

"I don't want to hurt you, Sunshine." He went back to his patio chair, pulled it around to face her, sat, and put his elbows on his knees. "I want to spend time with you, but usually when a man and woman start seeing each other, both understand that it could possibly lead to something. Love. Marriage. Children."

"Ah, so you really were only kidding about eloping. Bummer." She smiled, and her eyes softened. "Seriously, though, there's no way to know if after a week or a month or whatever, this chemistry is between us will fade and we go our separate ways, or if one or both of us will fall in love. If love comes into the equation, it sounds like one of us is going to get hurt. Probably me."

"Probably." Although he had a feeling this woman had the power to hurt him, and funny enough, he would be willing to risk it if she was agreeable to never having children. But he could never ask that of her.

"I've always wanted children someday, and I don't think I could give that dream up. I also don't want to give you up, Rand. So what do we do?"

Kinsey had only known this man what? About two weeks? She hadn't stopped to closely examine her feelings for him, but she had a sneaking suspicion that she was already falling for him. She got where he was coming from. If she'd experienced the kind of loss he had, she would likely be saying the same thing. As much as she wanted to keep seeing him, wouldn't it be wiser to end it now before she made the jump from falling for him to being in love with him? Or would she be willing to give up having children for this man?

She didn't have an answer.

"Maybe you should take some time to think," he said.

"That's a good idea." She wanted to cry at the sadness in his eyes. He'd had more pain in his life than anyone should have, and she wanted to crawl into his lap and soothe his hurts. She wanted to heal him. But she couldn't.

He smiled his sad smile as he stood. "I'm sorry, Kinsey."

"You have no reason to be." She held out her hand, letting him pull her up. She lifted onto her toes and placed a soft kiss on his lips. "I firmly believe those we've loved and lost are looking down on us. You said you've just recently been able to smile when thinking of Zoe. I think that makes her happy and that each time you do smile over a memory of her, she smiles, too."

"Jesus, Kinsey," he whispered. "There's nothing more

perfect you could have said just now. Thank you." He slid the back of his hand down her cheek. "You have my number. Call me when you make a decision."

"I will. Take care, Rand." After he was gone and she'd locked up behind him, she returned to the patio to think. She'd never seen a possibility of a future with Rick. All he'd been was someone to go out with, to have fun with. Rand was a different animal altogether. She could see herself falling in love with him, and that would only mean heartache because she didn't think she could give up having children. The tears came then, and with them came a sense that she'd lost something precious.

CHAPTER ELEVEN

FRIDAY CAME, THE NIGHT OF the Friends of the Library Ball. Rand thought it was a little strange that he'd rather be at Aces & Eights, considering he wasn't at all comfortable at the bar. He escorted Deidre Cummings into the Fontainebleau's grand ballroom, wishing he'd refused to be her escort when his father had asked. Even more, he wished it was Kinsey at his side.

He'd forgotten how glittery these things were. Ball gowns sparkled with crystals sewn in the bodices and skirts, competing for attention with diamonds flashing on fingers and necks. Across the room he saw his mother chatting up one of Miami's resident rock stars.

"Oh, there's Jonathan and Cynthia Johnstone. Do you know them?" Deidre asked.

"I do." He hadn't seen the Johnstones in over a year. Not surprising since this was the first function he'd attended since Olivia had left him. Jonathan was okay, but Cynthia was all about status and how much money was in one's bank account. He so badly didn't want to be here.

Deidre was lovely, blonde and blue-eyed, slim and pale. But she was made from the same mold as his ex-wife, and he couldn't help comparing her to the black-haired, brown-eyed beauty he couldn't stop thinking about. Apparently his taste in women had drastically changed.

"Rand Stevens, you do still exist," Jonathan said upon seeing him. He smiled at Deidre. "Hello, Deidre. How'd you get this guy to come out of whatever hole he's been hiding in?"

Deidre smiled back at Jonathan. "It's my superpower."

She and Cynthia air-kissed, then Rand got air-kisses from Cynthia. The hell, he hated these things. He spied his parents headed their way, and he braced himself, knowing his mother would bestow her own air-kisses on him before she found something to criticize.

"Hello, Randall," his mother said after almost touching her lips to first one cheek and then the other. "You've gained a few pounds. You should let me make you an appointment with my personal trainer."

"Regina, leave the boy alone." His father greeted Deidre and then Jonathan and Cynthia.

Well, that was embarrassing, having his mother chastise him in front of the others and then his dad calling him a boy. But that was the way it had always been, and he should be used to it by now. Nor had he gained weight, and was, in fact, in the best physical shape he'd ever been in due to Nate's insisting his agents spend time at the gym.

"Mother, you look beautiful, as usual," he said, not only because she expected the compliment but because it was true. Regina Stevens spent a lot of time and money to make sure she appeared a good ten or fifteen years younger in face and body than her fifty-five years. She graced him with a thin smile and then turned her attention to Deidre and Cynthia.

As a boy he'd vied for her attention in every way he could think of, but had never gotten more than a few words or an admonishment to behave. Somewhere around his early teens, he'd finally accepted that she didn't love him or his father. He still didn't understand why his dad stayed married to her, but that was a mystery he wasn't interested in solving.

Bored with the chitchat, he scanned the room, stilling when he locked eyes with the woman who'd been haunting his mind. A smile teased her lips at seeing him.

"Uh-oh. Marguerite Fletcher is wearing the same gown as Cynthia. That should liven things up when Cynthia notices," Deidre whispered, leaning against his arm.

Kinsey's gaze flicked from him to Deidre, and her smile froze, then faded away. She turned her face toward the man standing next to her. It was the same man who'd almost left bruises on her arm when he'd gone to Summer Fashions. Why the hell was she with him? Rand crushed the growl forming in this throat.

He glanced at Deidre to see her eyes dancing with mischief. She really was beautiful and amusing and nice. And she did absolutely nothing for him. There wasn't even the slightest hitch in his breath when her breasts brushed against his arm.

"So you're predicting fireworks as a part of tonight's entertainment?"

She gave a soft chuckle. "I've always loved fireworks."

As if his eyes had a mind of their own, they drifted back to Kinsey. She was watching them, but as soon as their gazes met, she looked away again. He knew exactly what she was thinking, that everything he'd said to her had been a lie.

And why was she with that douchebag?

"Who is she?"

Rand jerked his gaze away and turned to Deidre. "Who?"

"The woman you're staring so hard at. She's very pretty."

He almost said, *No one.* But that wasn't true. "Her name's Kinsey Landon."

"I see," she said, and he guessed she did because disappointment flashed in her eyes.

He was sorry for putting it there, but he had no intention of letting her think he'd be seeing her again. A waiter with a tray of champagne appeared, and after the others took a flute, he quietly asked for a club soda on ice with a lime. He'd learned that if he had one of those in his hand, people assumed it was a drink and wouldn't ask him questions he didn't want to answer.

His dad held out his arm. "Shall we go mingle, darling?" he asked his wife.

"Yes. I see Mayor Torres and his wife. We must say hello."

"They're a lovely couple," Deidre said after his parents wandered away.

Rand almost snorted. "Aren't they, though?" His parents, especially his mother, were very good at acting the loving couple when in public.

His gaze drifted back to Kinsey. She wore a black dress that hugged every delicious curve, but unlike the other women in the ballroom who were draped in diamonds and jewels, her only jewelry was a pair of silver dangling earrings and a silver comb holding one side of her hair above her ear. She was by far the most beautiful woman in the room, and she took his breath away.

It had been almost a week since he'd left her to think about them, if there was a them, and she hadn't called. He took that to be her answer. As much as it hurt—and the thought of not seeing her hurt a lot—he couldn't blame her.

The man she was with caught Rand watching them. Recognition flashed in his eyes, and he smirked. Holding Rand's gaze, the man trailed his fingers down Kinsey's arm. More than anything, Rand wanted to break those fingers.

"You should probably stop staring at them," Deidre whispered in his ear. "You're only encouraging him to piss you off."

Rand sputtered a laugh. He tore his gaze away from Kinsey. "Did you just say 'piss'?" Women of their world did not say words like *piss*.

She slyly smiled. "I know even naughtier words, Rand. You've pegged me as a clone of women like your ex-wife, and yes, I know Olivia. I was always a little rebel, much to my parents' chagrin." She darted a glance at Kinsey. "If she hadn't already stolen your heart, I think you and I could have rebelled together and had a shitload of fun doing it. But she has, and I don't settle for second best."

He didn't know what to say to that, but he decided he liked her, which he hadn't expected.

"Left you at a loss for words?" she said, amusement in her eyes. At his nod, she smirked. "I seem to have that effect on people. So, since we're not going to burn up the sheets together after our duty here is done, what can I do to help?"

"Help?" He was starting to sound like an idiot.

"Yep. I do love happy endings, and because I believe you're a good man, Rand Stevens, I think you should have yours. What's the problem? It's not that she doesn't want you. She can't stop sneaking peeks at you, and she doesn't like seeing you with me. So the reason the two of you are miserable because you're not together is…?"

"She wants children, and I don't." And why was he telling Deidre his personal problems?

"Ah, I see." She slipped her arm around his and pulled him over to a side wall, away from other people. "That's a hard problem to fix." Sympathy softened her eyes. "I have a tendency to stick my nose in other people's business, so forgive me if I'm stepping in where you don't want me."

When she paused, seeming to wait for him to tell her to either continue or shut up, he said, "And?" He wasn't sure why or even if he wanted to hear what she had to say, but he was curious enough to listen. If he'd met her before Olivia, he thought his life might have turned out entirely different.

"I hope I'm doing the right thing here." She glanced away, as if reconsidering, then met his gaze. "Okay, here it is. I met Olivia shortly after your divorce. A friend of mine who knew her invited her to have a girls' night out with us. After a few apple martinis Olivia got chatty, telling us about her divorce. She blamed it on you. She told us how your daughter died, said you couldn't get over it to the point that it was just too depressing to be around you."

Even though he knew Olivia blamed him for that very reason, anger heated his blood. How was he supposed to get over losing his baby girl? And how had it been so easy for Olivia to do just that?

"I had to about bite my tongue off to keep from calling her a cold bitch." She put her hand on his arm. "I'm going to share something very personal with you. I can't have children. The reason why isn't important, but if that gorgeous woman over there shooting daggers at me with her eyes because we're over here in the corner and I'm touching you hadn't already won your heart, I'd be the perfect woman for you." She chuckled. "That was an aside, not the message I'm trying to get across."

He couldn't help darting a glance at Kinsey. As soon as their eyes connected, she turned her back to him. He shifted his attention back to Deidre. "I'm not connecting the dots. Are you telling me to go after her or to forget her and choose you?"

She shook her head, wrinkling her nose at him. "I already told you I don't do second best. My point is, you knew the kind of love, a parent for a child, that I'll never get to experience. How can you deny yourself having that kind of love and joy in your life again? Is that what your daughter would want for you?"

"I don't—"

"I'm not finished. Quite honestly, I think you're being selfish. To her"—she tilted her head toward Kinsey—"and to the children you're not going to have because you're too afraid. Stop being a coward, Rand, and go yank your woman away from that asshole. As for me, I'm going to go talk to that cute bartender."

Stunned, Rand watched Deidre glide away. He wasn't being selfish, and he wasn't a coward. Was he? He slipped his hand into his pocket and touched Zoe's necklace. For a year he hadn't left the house without it in his pocket, as if it was a link to her. But it wasn't. It was just a necklace, a present he hadn't had a chance to give her.

Stop being a coward. Deidre's accusation echoed off the walls of his brain, growing louder with each bounce. "I'll always miss you, baby girl," he whispered, then let go of the necklace. As his gift for Zoe fell back into his pocket, a weight lifted, from his heart and from his soul. It was the first time he believed, really and truly believed, that he wouldn't betray his little girl by loving another child.

His gaze sought out Kinsey. She said something to the woman he'd left Kinsey's apartment keys with, and then she walked out of the ballroom. The man Kinsey had told him was the boss's son, the one Rand had the urge to kill, watched her leave. When she was out of sight, a look that was too cunning for Rand's comfort crossed his face as he eased away from his group and followed her.

C

Kinsey put her hands on the counter and closed her eyes. It had taken every ounce of her willpower and acting ability to stay in the ballroom and pretend she wasn't dying inside when she'd seen Rand with that woman. Whoever she was, she was stunning and everything that Kinsey wasn't. Willowy, blonde, blue-eyed, and a flawless creamy complexion. What her mother had always called peaches and cream. When her eyes refused to stop seeking him out, she'd fled to the restroom.

Considering his date tonight and the picture she'd seen of his wife, that was obviously the type of woman he preferred. She lifted her eyes to the mirror and studied her tan skin and body that definitely wasn't willowy. Had he only been toying with her, wanting a little taste of something different before he went back to the type of woman he preferred?

Every day for the past week she'd picked up her phone at least once an hour to call him, to tell him she wanted him no matter his conditions. Yet each time she'd paused, thinking of the children she'd never have if their relationship progressed to the point of marriage.

Seeing him tonight with another woman brought a revelation. She was in love with him. But in love enough to never hold her child in her arms? She could have him but no children or have children but not him. How was she supposed to choose between those two things?

It was too late, though, wasn't it? As hard as she'd tried not to watch him with the woman, her eyes ignored her wishes. They'd been cozy off by themselves, touching, their heads close together while deep in conversation. It hurt to see them together like that.

The restroom door opened, and she turned her back to whoever was coming in and grabbed a paper towel to wipe away the tears falling down her cheeks.

"Fancy meeting you here," Sebastian said, slipping his arms around her and pulling her against him.

"The hell, Sebastian. Get your hands off me." She tried to push his arms away, but he tightened them. He'd never scared her before, only creeped her out, but now she was frightened. There had to be a hundred women in the ballroom. You'd think one of them would need to use the restroom, but apparently not.

"Aw, come on, babe. Stop being a tease." He put his hand on her breast and squeezed.

"That hurts. If you don't get off me, I'm going to scream." She fisted her hand and tried to punch his face, but he laughed as her fist only grazed the side of his neck.

"Go ahead and fight me, little witch. That only turns me on more." He rocked his groin against her butt. "See how hard I am for you?"

Panicking now, she tried to twist around. If she could face him, she could knee him in the balls. He laughed, keeping a strong grip on her with his right arm. He circled her throat with the fingers of his left hand and squeezed tight enough to make it hard to breathe.

"You scream and it'll be the last sound you make. I'm tired of you teasing me." He rocked against her again. "I mean to get a piece of this sweet ass tonight. I've tried to be patient and romance you into my bed, but time's up, babe. I booked a room, so be a good little girl and come along quietly. If you try to call out to anyone, you'll be very sorry."

There wasn't a chance in hell that she was going anywhere with him. When he stuck his tongue in her ear, she thought she might vomit. She did the only other thing she could think of to do. She lifted her leg and aimed the spike of her shoe at his knee.

"Goddamn bitch! You'll pay for that."

Suddenly he was gone. He'd let go of her so fast that she stumbled forward, hitting her forehead hard on the wall. White stars blasted off behind her eyelids, and she sucked in a breath as excruciating pain throbbed through her head and down to her jaws. God, that hurt, but she'd freed herself from his hold, and now she had to get out before he got his hands on her again.

"I'm going to fucking kill you."

Rand? She turned and sagged against the wall. She blinked several times, trying to clear her vision. A blurry image of two men wrestling on the floor danced in front of her eyes. She tried to swallow, but that hurt, too.

The door opened, and a woman rushed in. Kinsey squinted. Oh, it was her, Rand's girlfriend. She added sadness to her pain, then gave in to the black void seeping into her head.

CHAPTER TWELVE

"**S**TOP IT, RAND. YOU'RE GOING to kill him."
Rand tried to shake off the hand that was tugging on his arm. He had every intention of killing the son of a bitch.

"Rand! Stop. Kinsey needs help."

Kinsey? At hearing her name, the bloodred rage that had taken over when he'd seen that hand around her throat lifted fractionally, just enough for him to see past the haze. To see her crumbled against the wall.

"Kinsey," he whispered. He looked down at the man he straddled. His nose was bleeding and appeared broken. His right eye was beginning to swell shut. Good. He deserved every bruise and more.

"You'll be sorry, asshole," the man grunted past a split lip. "My father—"

"You just tried to rape a woman, and then you assaulted an FBI agent. You have the right to remain silent, so not another word out of you." Rand swung his fist down one more time, knocking him out. He crawled over to Kinsey. "Sunshine, wake up." He wanted to pull her onto his lap, but he was afraid to move her. There was a large bump on her head from hitting the wall, and it was possible that she'd also hurt her neck. He growled at seeing the fingerprints on her skin.

Deidre leaned over his shoulder. "Is she going to be okay?"

He put two fingers on her neck, felt a strong pulse, and

breathed a sigh of relief. "For his sake, she better be."

"I'm sorry, but you can't come in right now."

Rand glanced over to see Deidre blocking whoever was trying to come in.

"You can't just hog the restroom," a female voice said.

"Actually I can," Deidre said, then put her back against the door and pushed it closed.

He had to get Kinsey help. "Is there a lock on the door?"

"Unfortunately, no." She huffed a breath, stiffening her back when the woman tried to push in again.

"Hold tight if you can." He retrieved his phone from his pocket and called his father. "I need you to come to the ladies room just outside the ballroom right now."

"On my way."

"Kinsey? Sweetheart, open your eyes." He rubbed his fingers over the top of her hand, afraid to touch her anywhere else. "Thank you," he said, glancing over at Deidre. "You had good timing."

She shook her head. "No, I saw her leave and him follow. Then when you headed after them, I thought there might be trouble. That you might need my help." She gave him a little shrug as if her actions were insignificant.

They weren't, and he owed her big. If not for her stopping him, he might well have killed the man in a blackened rage, but wanting to do it and actually doing it were two entirely different things.

A knock sounded at the door. "Rand?"

"That's my dad. Let him in."

"What's going on in there?" the same female voice loudly said.

"I'm wondering the same thing," Rand's father said after slipping into the room and pushing the door closed behind him. His gaze traveled the room, from the man out cold, to Rand, then to Rand's bleeding knuckles, and then to Kinsey. "Who's she?"

Rand glanced down at Kinsey, and then he lifted his eyes

to his father. "Someone very important to me."

"I see."

That was it, no other questions from his dad. Harlan Stevens was a take-charge man, one of the strengths that had made him very successful and rich, and he gave Rand a nod full of understanding.

"Deidre," he said, "I'm sorry if I or my son has put you in an uncomfortable situation, but I need you to stand outside the door and tell anyone who wants to come in that there is a medical emergency in here and they need to find another restroom."

"Okay." She put her hand on his father's arm. "And there's no reason to be sorry."

"That's good to hear. In a few minutes a man named Harrison will arrive. Tall, beefy, and black hair. Let him in."

"Got it." She slipped out.

Rand felt like he should be doing something, but he wouldn't leave Kinsey's side. She moaned and tried to move her head. He put his hands on each side of her neck, just below her hairline, to keep her still. "Easy, Sunshine. Help is on the way."

He listened as his dad called Harrison, his driver/bodyguard, instructing him on where to come. "And bring handcuffs," he said before ending the call.

Rand raised a brow at his father.

"He believes in always being prepared." Harlan punched some more numbers on his phone. "Greg, I need two private ambulances at the event where I am ASAP."

Greg was Harlan's secretary, had been for the past fifteen years, and the only one to last more than a few months.

"No, I'm not hurt. You're wasting time with your questions. Tell them to park behind the hotel and to come to the ladies room outside of the ballroom." He disconnected.

"Now, who's the man you took offense to and for what reason?"

"He's the son of her boss, and I think he tried to rape

her."

"Son of a bitch. He deserved a beating."

"I would have killed him, Dad, if Deidre hadn't stopped me."

"Then she has my gratitude. Even though he might deserve that, that would have been bad business."

Didn't he know it. He'd put his job on the line tonight, but he couldn't find it in him to care. All that mattered was Kinsey.

"I'm here," Harrison said, coming into the room.

"Put handcuffs on that bastard over there," Harlan said, pointing at Sebastian. "Son, what's the plan here? He needs to be arrested and charged with attempted rape." He studied Kinsey. "And assault."

"I need to call my boss. This is Kinsey Landon, Nate's sister."

"Well, shit. Those Gentry boys aren't going to take kindly to someone hurting their sister."

"No, they aren't." He wasn't taking so kindly to it either.

Deidre stuck her head in. "The press assigned to cover the gala is out here wanting to know what's going on."

"Harrison."

That was all his dad had to say to have his bodyguard heading out to take control.

"Hurts."

Rand jerked his gaze to Kinsey. Thank you, God, she was awake. "Hey, Sunshine, welcome back." He thought he might be able to breathe again.

Her eyes were cloudy, which was concerning. And the one word she'd said had sounded raspy in the way damaged vocal cords would.

"Hurts," she said again in that scratchy voice that made him wish he could get another go at the man who'd hurt her.

"What hurts, baby?"

"Head. Throat. Neck." All three words sounded as

if they'd been an effort for her to say. Her gaze fell on her attacker. She made a sound that reminded him of a wounded animal as she tried to disappear into the wall.

"Kinsey, listen to me. You're safe. You are safe."

Her eyes met his, and as if she saw the truth in his words, she smiled. She fucking smiled at him after what had been done to her. After he'd failed to protect her. Damn him to hell and back for that smile he didn't deserve.

Deidre was right. He'd been a coward. But no more. If Kinsey didn't turn her back on him after this, he'd fall to his knees in gratitude. If she wanted babies, he'd give her however many dozens of them she wanted. If that scared him down to his toes, he'd somehow deal with it. For her.

The next minutes passed in a blur as he let his father take over so he could stay with Kinsey until help arrived. Harlan somehow managed to clear the hallway leading to the women's room, get the bastard—Rand still didn't know his name, but he'd find out—who had hurt Kinsey sent off in one ambulance and Kinsey in another, both to a private hospital Rand had never heard of.

Rand was riding in the ambulance carrying the man to make sure he didn't cause trouble. As much as he'd rather be with Kinsey, he was the only one with a badge since he didn't want to involve the police until he talked to Nate. His father and Deidre were following in Harlan's limo, and as soon as Harrison dropped Harlan off at the hospital, he would take Deidre home. After doing that, he'd return to the gala to wait until Rand's mother was ready to leave.

Rand made a mental note to send Deidre flowers, along with a message of appreciation for all her help. She'd turned out to be pretty amazing, and he now counted her as a friend.

He needed to call Nate, but he didn't want to talk in front of his prisoner or the EMT. As soon as they arrived, he told his father to stand guard in the emergency room, then went to make sure Kinsey was getting immediate attention. Once he confirmed that she was, he walked outside and made the call he dreaded.

"It's Rand," he said when Nate answered.

"So my caller ID claims. I thought you were wining and dining with the beautiful people tonight."

"I was until… until I almost beat a man to death."

"Just what kind of gala does the Friends of the Library put on? You need me to come bail you out of jail?"

"No. I'm at Doctors of Healing Hospital. Nate, the man I almost killed, wanted to kill, tried to rape your sister."

"The hell you say. Is she hurt?"

"Yes. Probably a concussion, maybe a neck injury. The doctor's with her now."

"I'm on the way."

The line went dead. He went back inside and found his father leaning against the wall where he could keep an eye on the curtained-off room where they had Kinsey's attacker handcuffed to a bed. "Anything on Kinsey yet?"

"Yes, they took her up to X-ray. They wanted to get some pictures of her head and neck. The doctor said he'd talk to her family when they arrived."

Rand thrust a thumb toward the curtain. "What about him?"

"He's making noises. Wants to file assault charges against you. Says his father is going to sue you for everything you own. I've already called my lawyer, and he's on standby should we need him."

"He can come at me all he wants. He has no idea who he's messing with. Nate will be here shortly, most likely with his brothers in tow. When they see their sister, they'll probably be pissed I didn't kill him."

"Do you know who he is?"

"Not his name, but he's the son of the owner of Summer Fashions, the place Kinsey works."

"Jacob Summer owns it." He took out his phone. "Greg, I want everything you can find on Jacob Summer, owner of Summer Fashions. I especially want whatever you can dig up about his son."

"Dad, we're perfectly capable of investigating him, and believe me, if there's any dirt on him, we'll find it," Rand said after his father disconnected.

"I know, but Greg can... how should I say this considering I'm talking to an FBI agent? Let's just say he doesn't have to worry about the legalities of his snooping. Now tell me about this woman who's very important to you."

"She's the sister the Gentry brothers didn't know about until recently." He gave his father an abbreviated version of the story. "I didn't know she was their sister in the beginning or I never would have gone near her. It figures that the first woman to catch my interest since Olivia turned out to be the sister of three overly protective males."

"They have a problem with you seeing her?"

Rand had to smile at his father taking offense that the Gentrys might have a problem with his son. "Stand down. It's not personal. They'd have a problem with any man getting near her."

"You called her Sunshine."

"Because that's what she's brought into my life."

"Son, I've been worried that you'd never let yourself be happy again. If that woman is the reason for bringing the light back into your eyes, then she's special as far as I'm concerned."

"Yeah, she is." He just hoped he hadn't blown it with her. "And here they come," he said, seeing the sliding door open and Nate striding in. Not only had he brought Court and Alex with him, but Taylor and Madison, too. He assumed that the only reason Lauren wasn't here was because she was due to deliver just about any day.

"Where is she?" Nate demanded.

"Upstairs in X-ray."

"Start at the beginning."

The brothers and their wives crowded around him.

Keeping his voice low so their prisoner couldn't overhear, he told them what happened, leaving Deidre out of it. There was no reason to bring this mess into her life since she hadn't witnessed the attack. When he finished, Nate stared at him for a moment with narrowed eyes.

"You're being a little fuzzy on a few details, intentionally, I think. Where were you when you saw him follow her out of the ballroom?"

And this was where the brothers were going to chew a piece of his ass. "I was across the room." He'd hoped to skirt around this part because it was only going to confirm their belief that they didn't want him anywhere near Kinsey.

"Why? If she was your date, you should have been with her."

"She wasn't my date."

"So you attended the gala solo and she just happened to be there, too?"

"No, I was with someone else. It appeared that Kinsey was here with her boss and coworkers."

Nate's black eyes went from narrowed to slitted, giving Rand the impression of a viper about to strike. "You have my..." He glanced at the other members of his family. "Our gratitude for stopping him from hurting her even more than he did, but this is where you step away."

"Nate, that's Kinsey's decision," Taylor said.

"No, it isn't."

Both Taylor and Madison gave him sympathetic looks, and he appreciated it, but it was the brothers he was going to have to deal with if he wanted to keep seeing Kinsey. And he did. More than ever.

Rand stiffened his spine and lifted his shoulders. "What happens between Kinsey and me is between Kinsey and me." If she wanted to share what had been said between them, that was up to her. As far as he was concerned, it was none of their business.

"We're her family," Court said. "We have the right to protect her, and if that means keeping you from hurting her, we will do that."

"If you think my son will hurt your sister, you're delusional. His date was one I set up for him, not knowing that he—"

"Dad." Rand shook his head. Although he understood his father not liking the way this conversation was going, it was his battle to fight. "Why don't you call Harrison to come get you? I appreciate all you did tonight more than you can imagine, but it's time for you to go."

"It probably is. I stick around much longer and I'm going to knock some sense into these boys." He squeezed Rand's shoulder. "I'm proud of you, son. When I hear from Greg, I'll call you." He nodded at Nate, then walked away.

Alex watched him leave before shifting his gaze to Rand. "I would have given anything to have a father like yours." He glanced at his brothers. "All of us would have. That tells me you were raised right. I also think there's a lot you're not saying about things you and Kinsey have talked about. And you're right. Those things are between the two of you."

"Alex," Nate warned.

"*Nate*," Alex mocked. "That he was even keeping an eye on her while he was with someone else tells me something. The minute Kinsey says she doesn't want to see him, he'll see her over my dead body. Until then, who attacked her? Because that's where our attention should be, along with what are we going to do about it? I vote for teaching him a lesson he'll never forget."

Court let out a sigh. "I hate it when Alex's right."

Rand's phone vibrated, and at seeing his father's name on the screen, he clicked on answer. "Yeah?" His gaze skimmed over the brothers as he listened. They weren't going to like what his dad had learned any more than he did. "Thanks. Now tell Greg to stop nosing around."

He slipped his phone back into his pocket. "His name's Sebastian Summer, son of Jacob Summer, the owner of Summer Fashions. He—"

"That has to be who she said was bothering her," Court said.

Taylor frowned. "He was bothering her before tonight?"

"Yeah," Nate said, nodding. "She mentioned it, then told us to back off, that she could handle him. Our mistake was agreeing."

"She had no reason to think he was anything more than a nuisance. If she'd known what my father just told me, she would have handled things differently." He'd witnessed the man bothering her and hadn't done anything about it, assuming the same thing. That didn't sit well with him. "Seems Sebastian Summer has a history of stepping over the line where women are concerned. He was expelled from high school for spying on girls in the locker room. In college a student reported him to administration for sexually harassing her. He was reprimanded, then when a second female student reported him, he was expelled."

"How did your father find that out so fast?" Madison said.

"Don't ask."

"That might be only the tip of the iceberg." Court glanced at Nate. "I'll start digging into his background when I get home tonight."

Put Court in front of a computer and there wasn't anything he couldn't find. Before they were through with Sebastian Summer, he was going to wish he'd never touched Kinsey.

"Are any of you Kinsey Landon's family?" a man in scrubs asked, walking up to them.

"Yes, we are," Nate said. "How is she?"

"She has a mild concussion, a bruised larynx, and whiplash. None of those are life-threatening, and she will completely recover. I want to keep her overnight so we can observe her, but I'm confident that we'll be able to release her in the morning. She'll need to rest for a week, especially her voice."

"We'll make sure of it." Nate pulled his badge out of his pocket and held it open for the doctor to see. "Nate Gentry, special agent in charge of the Miami field office. The man brought in when she was is Sebastian Summer. When will he be released?"

"His face is a mess, but I can release him now."

"No. I want him held overnight, no visitors and no phone calls. Put him in a room by himself. I'll have an agent here to stand guard. If Mr. Summer makes any demands, my agent will deal with him."

"Why don't I just give him something to make him sleep until tomorrow?"

"Even better. I'll still have an agent here to keep an eye on him, though. When can we see our sister?"

"In a few minutes. We're taking her to a room now and getting her settled in."

After the doctor left, Nate turned to Rand. "So you messed up his face?"

"I did." And he wasn't sorry.

Nate gave him a curt nod. "Good. You can go now. We'll take it from here."

"No. Not until I see Kinsey."

CHAPTER THIRTEEN

KINSEY SIGHED AFTER THE NURSE left. She hated not being able to talk. No one was telling her what was going on. Where was Rand? She knew he'd been in the emergency room because she'd heard him talking. Had he left? Had anyone called her brothers? This was going to be all the ammunition they needed to justify meddling in her life.

And what about Sebastian? Where was he? Hopefully in jail, but since no one was telling her anything, as far as she knew he could be sitting at home by now, planning his next attack. She shuddered. Until tonight she'd just thought he was a creep, but one she could handle. What if he was roaming the hallways right now, looking for her? Her heart skipped a beat.

The room suddenly seemed too quiet. She slid down on the bed and pulled the cover up to her chin. Her mother had always said she had a vivid imagination, and right now it was working overtime. She could visualize the door creaking open, could see Sebastian sneaking in to finish what he'd started. She glanced around, looking for something she could use as a weapon.

"There's nothing," she rasped, forgetting she wasn't supposed to talk. Her throat burned in protest, and she reached for the glass of water on the table. As she sipped, she realized she could throw the glass at his face, so she held on to it after she was done drinking. And the TV remote. She could throw that, too. Or even better, shove it into his throat, see how he liked not being able to talk. Now she had two weapons, and if—

The door eased open, sending her heart into jack-hammer mode. She tightened her grips on the glass and remote, ready to use them. When Nate appeared, she was so relieved that she almost dropped the glass of water.

"Hey," he said, walking in. Court, Alex, Taylor, and Madison followed him into the room.

Tears burned her eyes that they were all here for her. She waved her fingers at them. They crowded around her bed, and she wished she could speak so she could tell them how much it meant to her that they'd come. Nate made a growling sound, and she looked up to see his eyes focused on her throat. She'd gone to the bathroom when they'd brought her to the room and had seen the fingerprints on her skin.

"Oh, sweetie," Madison said. "Look what he did to you."

Her brothers exchanged glances, and she guessed they were plotting Sebastian's demise.

Taylor brushed Kinsey's hair back. "Is there anything you need or want us to get you?"

She picked up the pen and notepad the nurse had left her and wrote one word.

Sebastian?

"Handcuffed to a bed on a different floor with one of my agents standing guard," Nate said.

Alex leaned over and gently kissed her forehead. "Isn't a kiss supposed to make a boo-boo better?" He grinned when she nodded.

"Just so you know, the next time some man is bothering you, we won't be standing aside," Court said.

Good she wrote.

Taylor sat on the edge of the mattress. "Lauren stayed home with the kids, but she sends her love."

She wrote some more. *Thank you. It means so much to me that you all are here, but you don't have to stay. I'm okay. Really.*

Not really, but it was late and she wouldn't ask them to stay.

Nate put his hand on Taylor's shoulder. "Here's the plan. Court has some things to do tonight, so he's heading home. Taylor and I are meeting with the police to arrange the arrest of Mr. Summer. Alex and Madison are going to stay with you tonight."

Damn tears.

"Rand wants to see you, but that's up to you."

He's here?

Alex snorted. "Pacing outside your door like a caged lion. But like Nate said, if you don't want to see him, we'll send him away."

Want to thank him.

She didn't even want to think what would have happened if he hadn't stopped Sebastian.

"Do you want us to stay when he comes in?" Court asked.

After thinking about it a moment, she shook her head. She needed to know if Rand had meant the things he'd said to her, and if so, who was the woman with him? It was a conversation she didn't want her brothers butting their noses into.

Court squeezed her hand. "I'm heading out. Get some rest, and I'll see you tomorrow."

She waved her fingers at him, mouthing, *Okay.*

"Do you want Nate and me to run by your apartment and get you some clothes and toiletries?" Taylor asked.

Kinsey gave a vigorous nod to that. She pointed at Taylor. Thinking of Nate digging around in her underwear drawer made her cheeks heat.

Apparently reading her mind, Taylor laughed. "Trust me, he'd turn redder than you are right now if he had to pack your undies."

"Truth," Nate said, but she saw the amusement in his eyes. "I'll leave your unmentionables in her capable hands."

She seriously doubted anything would embarrass him, but he'd made her smile. It struck her as weird that she was smiling after what had happened, but it felt good. The nurse had left a plastic bag on the table next to the bed with her clothes and purse. She retrieved her clutch and fished out her house key, giving it to Taylor.

After she was left with Alex and Madison, Alex said, "We'll be right outside while you talk to Rand."

She gave him a thumbs-up. Knowing she was about to see Rand, her heart rate decided to misbehave by accelerating from zero to sixty in less than the time it took for him to walk in. God help her, just the sight of him had her ovaries begging to have his babies. And that right there was the problem. Or so she'd thought until seeing him with another woman. That had slayed her.

"Hey, Sunshine." He pulled a chair next to the bed and sat.

The last thing she felt like right now was sunshine, but she forced a smile.

"Christ, Kinsey, I'm so sorry I didn't get to him sooner. Before he hurt you."

She picked up the notepad and pen.

Not your fault.

He read the note, but she could tell by the regret in his eyes that he still blamed himself, which was silly. The only person to blame was Sebastian. She pointed to the words she'd written. Not being able to talk was irritating.

His smile was sad. "If I hadn't been so stupid, you would have been my date for the gala and this never would have happened."

What was he saying? She tamped down on the hope trying to take hold in her heart.

Stupid?

"Yeah." He glanced away, then returned his gaze to her. "I realized something tonight. Well, to give credit where it's due, Deidre said some things that opened my eyes to what a big mistake I was making."

Even her name was pretty. Kinsey had never known jealousy before, and it wasn't a feeling she liked. She didn't know where he was going with this, so she waited, but the hope that had tried to blossom died. Deidre was not only beautiful, she was from his world. He'd never said so, but it hadn't been hard to figure out that he was rich, and he didn't get that way from working for the FBI. He had to have come from money, and how was she supposed to compete with a woman who obviously had more in common with him than she did?

"Just so you know, my father set up the date with her without telling me until after the fact. She noticed that I couldn't take my eyes off you tonight, and she asked who you were. Somehow it all came out, how much I wanted you. That you wanted children, and why I wouldn't consider it. She told me I was being selfish, not only to myself but to you. And she was right."

Kinsey decided she might like Deidre after all.

"I just hope that I didn't figure all this out too late."

Her heart soared, lifting off like a rocket bound for the stars. She covered her notepad so he couldn't see what she was writing. When she finished, she handed it to him.

For you it's never too late. I love you.

She watched for his reaction. He read the note, then lifted eyes to hers that were bright and happy.

"God, Kinsey. I love you like crazy." He glanced around them, then pushed her pad and pen away and took her hand in his. "A hospital room isn't how I would have wanted to tell you, but I'll make it up to you. As soon as you're better, we'll have a romantic dinner at the best restaurant, and we'll pretend I'm telling you for the first time."

She pulled her hand away and grabbed the pen and paper.

A hamburger will work just as well.

Rand laughed, his heart filled with love for this woman. "We'll do that, too. But only the best for my girl, whether it's a hamburger or a fancy dinner." He'd been afraid to hope that he still had a chance with her.

She wrote something again, then handed it to him.

You really are okay with having children?

"With you, yes. I'll probably worry over everything, maybe even keep them isolated in a germ-free room." He grinned when she widened her eyes. "Just kidding. I think. Seriously, I probably will be overprotective. One sneeze and we'll be off to the doctor, but I have faith that you can talk me off the ledge."

She wrote again.

Anytime you're about to walk off the ledge, I'll just take you to bed.

He was pretty sure his grin stretched from ear to ear. "That'll work. But listen. Let's not talk marriage and babies right now. You need to rest. After you're well, we'll take some time to just enjoy each other. I might have told you I love you in a hospital room, but the hell if I'm going to ask you to marry me in one."

"Oh," she rasped. Her eyes widened, and a beautiful smile appeared on her face. She tapped her finger against her lips, then puckered them.

"Are you asking for a kiss?" At her vigorous nod, he moved to the edge of the bed. "Whatever my lady wants," he said in a bad British accent, smiling when she rolled her eyes.

They'd kissed before, but as their mouths connected, he knew this one would be different. New. He rested his hand on her neck and gently caressed her cheek with his thumb. Their breaths mingled when their lips touched, and Jesus God, this woman. His sunshine. His salvation.

"Kinsey," he breathed. The kiss was their promise of a new beginning, of a life together. Passion sizzled between them as his tongue delved into her mouth, and when he heard her soft sigh, he reminded himself that they were in a hospital room, that she was hurt.

He reluctantly pulled away. "You need to get some rest. I'll be right here if you need me."

You don't have to stay, she wrote.

"Yes, I do. I need to be here." What if she had a nightmare? Or needed to talk about what had happened at three in the morning? "Now close your eyes, Sunshine." He dimmed the lights, then settled in his chair. She was asleep before a minute passed, which didn't surprise him. It had been a long night, and she had to be tired.

As he sat in the darkened room, watching her sleep, he marveled at how much his life had changed since the moment she'd walked into Aces & Eights. If he'd known she was the Gentrys' sister, he wouldn't have gone near her. Thank God he hadn't. After he was sure she was sleeping soundly, he eased out of the room to tell Alex and Madison he was staying and they could go home.

Alex was on his phone, and from his expression, Rand could tell something was wrong. "You should have killed him," were the first words out of his mouth after he disconnected.

"Summer?"

"What happened?" Madison asked.

"While Taylor was gathering a few things to bring Kinsey, Nate was looking around and noticed a reflection of the overhead light coming from an artificial tree in the corner of Kinsey's bedroom."

"A fucking camera?" Most people didn't realize that a spy camera lens, even a small one, reflected light. And most people weren't observant enough to notice they were being spied on.

"Yeah. So he and Taylor started searching for more. They've found three so far. The one in the bedroom, aimed at her bed, one in the bathroom, and one in the living room."

Madison gasped. "My God."

Rage blew through Rand's bloodstream with the speed

of an EF5 tornado. How long had they been there? He remembered the night she'd finally decided she'd left her back door cracked open. Had that been when he'd put them in her apartment? Had the bastard been watching her all this time?

"He's a dead man," he growled.

Anger shimmered in Alex's eyes. "We can't be sure yet it was him, but who else would it be? Court's on his way to her place. He'll be able to trace the cameras back to their source."

"We both know it will go straight to Summer."

Alex nodded. "Yeah, and that just gives us more to charge him with. Before Court left for Kinsey's, he was able to confirm what your dad already told you. He's confident there's more to be found, but with his attack on Kinsey and the spying on her, he's going down. We're also going to charge him with assault on a federal agent." Alex narrowed his eyes. "You did identify yourself, right?"

Eff him. He could easily say he had. It would be his word against a man who preyed on women, so a justified lie? But he couldn't look Alex in the eyes and lie to the man. "I told him I was FBI after I had him subdued."

Alex put his hands over Madison's ears. "Semantics, dude. Things happened so fast, it's hard to remember the time-line. But you do remember that you left him no doubt you were a federal agent?"

"What he said," Madison said, pushing her husband's hands away.

"I absolutely remember leaving him in no doubt as to who I was when I was arresting him." He got where Alex was coming from, and who was to say at what point he'd tried to put the man under arrest? If he had a hair's breadth of doubt that Sebastian Summer was innocent, he would have no choice but to tell the truth. He wasn't exactly lying; he was only fudging a little on the timeline. To make sure Kinsey was protected from ever having Sebastian

Summer hurt her again, he would fudge his fucking life away with no regrets.

So that was what real love felt like.

CHAPTER FOURTEEN

THE LAST THING KINSEY HAD seen when closing her eyes against the pain and the replay of the attack in her mind had been Rand's face. And she thought knowing he was with her was the only reason she'd been able to sleep. He would keep her safe. The first thing she saw when waking up was Rand's face. Well, not really his face because he was doing a face-plant on her thigh.

She eased her hand onto his head, hoping that she didn't wake him. She needed a few minutes of quiet time to think about the things he'd said to her last night, but he shot up as if she'd banged cymbals next to his ears.

"Kinsey?" He blinked his eyes, then scrubbed a hand over his face.

"You need to shave." She wanted to slap a hand over her mouth. Her brothers wore scruff better than any men she'd ever seen, but Rand was meant to be clean-shaven. That was his most beautiful look. Not this face that seemed as if he'd aged a thousand years in one night because of her.

Oh, and she could talk. That was awesome. She didn't have to try to write her thoughts anymore.

He gave her a smile that curled her toes. "Good morning, Sunshine."

"You're still here," she whispered back.

"Like I'd be anywhere else."

"I want to go home."

"The doctor will be here shortly. As soon as he releases you, I'll spring you from this joint." He tapped her nose with his finger. "Your voice still sounds a little scratchy, so try not to talk too much. Let it get some rest."

She stuck her tongue out, grinning when he laughed. But her throat was still sore, so she did need to let it rest.

"Nate and Taylor dropped off some clothes and stuff for you."

What she wanted the most right now was her toothbrush. She also wanted to know if Sebastian had been arrested yet, but that conversation would have to wait since the doctor walked into the room.

An hour later she was in Rand's car, but he wasn't headed in the direction of her apartment. "Where are we going?" The doctor had said she could talk, but that she should save her voice as much as possible for the next few days. Her head still hurt, but not as much as it had last night, thankfully.

"To the field office. Your brothers want to talk to you."

Cool. She'd love to see where they worked. He reached across the console, picked up her hand, brought it to his mouth, and kissed her fingers. Instead of letting go, he lowered both their hands to his thigh, keeping his on top of hers.

How was it possible that everything with him seemed familiar, as if they were completely in tune, yet felt new? She turned her hand over, threading her fingers around his. He'd told her he loved her last night, but he hadn't said it this morning. In fact, he appeared preoccupied, as if something was on his mind. Did he regret those words?

"What are you thinking about so hard over there?"

Her first reaction was to shrug off his question, but if they really were going to have a relationship, they needed to be honest with each other. "What you said last night, did you mean it?"

"That I love you?" She nodded. He squeezed her hand. "Yes, I meant every word. I wasn't looking to fall in love, and I don't know how it happened, but it did. Tell me you're not having second thoughts."

"No." Not even. "I love you. I do. But you've just been really quiet today, so I wondered if you were the one having second thoughts."

He glanced over at her and winked. "Not a one, Sunshine. There are some things you need to know, but we'll talk about those when we sit down with your brothers."

That sounded ominous.

☾

Kinsey was disappointed in the FBI's field office. She'd expected something like out of one of her favorite TV shows, *NCIS*. But there weren't any fancy gadgets that she could see. It looked like a normal office with cubicles and desks.

"Hmph."

"You say something?" Rand asked as he led her through the room.

"Just thinking out loud."

He eyed her for a moment, then grinned. "You're disappointed. You thought it would be something like out of a James Bond movie."

"Close." And how did he do that, read her so well?

"Sorry, but nothing fancy here." He put his arm around her shoulders. "Hopefully this won't take long, and then we can get you… ah, somewhere you can rest for the day."

She didn't like the sound of that. "My own bed is where I can rest." She also didn't like when he didn't respond, giving her the impression plans had been made for her that she wasn't aware of. But a day to rest was definitely on her agenda. Maybe by tomorrow her headache would be gone and she could start worrying about finding a job since there was no way she could return to Summer Fashions.

The conference room was empty when they entered. After pulling out a chair for her along the middle of the table, he walked to a small refrigerator against the wall and returned with two bottles of water. Her scratchy throat welcomed the cold liquid. A minute later Taylor and her brothers came in.

"Dudes," she said in greeting.

Next to her, Rand groaned. "Not you, too."

She winked at Alex when he laughed. During the cook-out at Nate's, she'd noticed that *dude* was not one of Rand's favorite words.

Alex came around to her side of the table, sitting next to her. Taylor, Nate, and Court sat across from her. All their gazes fell on her face as if scrutinizing her injuries. She managed not to squirm.

"You look a bit better than you did last night, little sister," Alex said.

"I feel better." She glanced at Taylor. "Thanks for getting me some clothes, and especially for sending my toothbrush along. My mouth felt like a cotton field this morning."

"I wish the reason I had to didn't exist, but you're welcome."

"So, what's on your minds? I'd really like to go home and crawl into bed."

Nate shook his head. "You're not going back to that apartment. Ever."

"Whoa! You don't get to decide that." Her mind was sluggish today or she would have realized that was what this little meeting was going to be about. "Just because you're my oldest brother, which I guess makes you the head of the family, doesn't mean—"

"How about this then? We found three cameras in your apartment. He's been spying on you, Kinsey. Even with them gone, are you going to feel comfortable there again?"

"What?" Her stomach took a sickening roll. "How do you know this?"

"Because Nate found the cameras and I've linked into the feed," Court said, and she didn't like how his eyes stayed focused on the table instead of him looking at her.

She lifted her gaze to Rand's. "How long were cameras in my apartment?"

"Remember the night you thought you left your back door open? We think he installed them then. Maybe he got careless about leaving the back door open, or you got home earlier than expected and surprised him, so he left in a hurry."

"He's been watching me?"

Court nodded. "Yeah."

She shuddered. Just the thought of Sebastian watching her made her feel as if someone had lit her insides on fire. Beads of sweat rolled down her back. Rand reached for her hand, but she didn't want to be touched. She pushed away from the table.

"Bathroom?"

"I'll show you," Taylor said.

As soon as she walked into the restroom, she went straight to the sink and turned on the water. It was cold, but not cold enough. She wanted it to feel like ice on her face. She wanted freezing numbness. After she'd soaked the top half of her shirt trying to wash away any thought of Sebastian and what he'd done, she twisted off the faucet handle.

It hadn't worked. Not only had he left her feeling dirty, but he'd taken everything from her. Her sense of security, her job, and her apartment because she could never live there again.

"Here, sweetie." Taylor handed her a couple of paper towels. "You can't let that creep mess with your head."

"And how is that supposed to work?" The dam broke, and the tears Kinsey had been holding back flowed down her cheeks. "I feel so violated." Taylor opened her arms, and Kinsey walked into her sister-in-law's embrace.

"Try not to think about that right now," Taylor said, combing her fingers through Kinsey's hair. "Ready to go back in and get this over with so you can get out of here?"

Kinsey sighed. "I don't want to. I just can't deal with all

of this right now." It felt good to have family to comfort her. What if this had happened before she found her brothers, when she'd still been alone? That didn't bear thinking about.

"Okay then. Come with me."

She followed Taylor into another room and, at the sight of a leather couch, headed straight to it.

"This is Nate's office. No one will bother you in here. I'm going to fix you a cup of tea, then go tell the guys that I'm taking you home with me."

"Thank you."

"Sweetie, you're family. We take care of our own, no thanks necessary."

❦

Rand pushed his chair back, intending to follow Kinsey. She was clearly distraught, not that he blamed her. Knowing Summer had watched them made him want to hurt something, specifically Sebastian Summer.

"Stay," Nate said. "Taylor will take care of her."

That was his job. But she'd fled when he'd tried to take her hand to let her know that he was here for her. He reluctantly settled back into his chair. "She'll stay with me." On that he was resolute. If her brothers whisked her away to their compound, who knew when he'd get to see her again? He was the one she needed, the one who could and would help her get through this.

Nate shook his head. "No, she needs her family right now."

"I'm in love with her, so that makes me her family, too."

"How did that happen?"

He managed not to roll his eyes at Nate. "How did you happen to fall in love with Taylor?"

"She didn't give me any choice."

"There you go."

"She loves him, too," Alex said.

Court smirked at his brother. "You're such a romantic, baby brother. You want everyone to love everyone."

"So sue me if I want to see the people I care about happy."

"He's right, though," Rand said. "She told me last night at the hospital that she loved me." He sat forward, putting his hands flat on the table. "When I first met her, I didn't know she was your sister. If I had, I wouldn't have gone near her, but truthfully I'm glad I didn't know. I get that you want to take care of her, but so do I. And I'm not backing down on this."

Court tapped his fingers on the arm of his chair. "Why don't we table a decision on where Kinsey goes for a few minutes? I need to bring you up to speed on what I've found on Summer before she comes back. Hearing it would only upset her more."

"Fine," Nate said, giving Rand a dark look before turning his attention to Court. "Talk."

"You already know about his expulsions from high school and college. Jacob Summer has twice, that I've found so far, paid off women to keep quiet about his son. Both were employees of Summer Fashions who'd filed sexual harassment charges against him with EEOC. They were later dropped."

"Money change hands?" Rand asked.

"Yep. I was able to get both of them on the phone this morning. One said she'd signed an agreement not to talk about it and refused to say more. That confirmed that she'd received money. The second was very chatty, even though she admitted that she'd also signed an agreement. She regrets that she let Jacob Summer coerce her into dropping the charges against his son. She didn't want to, but he said if she didn't, he would ruin her life, that she'd never be able to get another job. Then there's one more woman I haven't been able to reach. A third employee who filed a sexual assault charge with the police. That was also dropped, so

I'm guessing his father got to her, too."

Rand fisted his hands. He didn't know the women's circumstances and didn't blame them for caving in to a bully, but if they'd not backed off their claims, Kinsey might have been spared Summer's attention.

"Did you get the police report for that one?" Rand asked. Court darted a glance at Nate, and Rand got the impression that he was worried about the reaction to the answer from the special agent in charge of the FBI's Miami field office.

"Yeah, he attacked her in the bathroom at Summer Fashions."

"The fuck," Nate said.

"I want to kill him," Rand said. If Sebastian Summer was in front of him right now, he wouldn't have any qualms about carrying out that threat. And he'd very much like five minutes in a room with Jacob Summer.

"The police took him into custody early this morning," Nate said. "I was there to observe the detective in charge of the case question him. At first Summer denied everything, but when confronted with the list of witnesses, especially that one was an FBI agent, he admitted to following Kinsey into the bathroom. He claims she asked him to, but then changed her mind about wanting to have sex with him. According to him, he was leaving when a man attacked him for no reason. All bullshit, of course, and with Kinsey's testimony and yours, Rand, along with her injuries, he's not going to get out of this one. His past history will also work against him."

Rand had thought he already hated the man to full capacity, but he was wrong. "Did he admit to breaking into her apartment and planting the cameras?"

"Not at first, but when the detective told him his fingerprints were on the cameras, he claimed it was a game Kinsey wanted to play, a fantasy of being watched that she wanted to act out. She had a habit of leaving her keys on her desk, and he had a copy made. Because she supposedly left her keys for him to find, he wasn't really breaking in."

Alex stood, went to the window, and looked out. "He's a sick bastard. We can make him disappear without a trace," he said, giving them his back. "But as much as we'd like to, we won't."

"No, we won't, but I've never been so tempted to take matters into my own hands before." Rand pulled a pen out of the cup in the center of the table that held a dozen or so of them. He flicked it a few times, then broke it in half. "What we can do is put this piece of shit in prison for so long that his dick doesn't remember what a woman looks like by the time he gets out."

"That we can do," Court agreed.

Nate nodded. "And will. He'll come in front of a judge tomorrow. I've already talked to the DA, and they're going to ask for the maximum bail. This afternoon I'm going to talk to his father and see if I can discourage him from paying it."

Rand dropped the broken pen onto the table. "Hopefully Daddy's getting tired of bailing him out of trouble."

"What have I missed?" Taylor said after walking into the room and coming to stand behind her husband, putting her hands on his shoulders.

Nate reached up and covered her hands with his. "I'll catch you up later. Where's Kinsey?"

"In your office. She's hurt and embarrassed." She gave Rand a sad smile. "I'm taking her home for a girls' afternoon with me, Lauren, and Madison."

Rand stood. "No, she's coming with me. I'll check in with you later tonight, after she's asleep." He walked out before anyone could argue.

CHAPTER FIFTEEN

"SHOWER, BATH, OR BED?"

Kinsey forced a smile. "A bath sounds wonderful." Without giving her a chance to refuse, Rand had whisked her off to his place. Truthfully she was glad the decision had been taken from her.

As much as she was learning to love her brothers and their families, she couldn't imagine their homes would be nice and quiet with all the children around. And that was what she craved. She wanted to crawl into a bed and pull the covers over her head, shutting everyone and everything out. But first she wanted to feel clean. If that was at all possible. She wasn't sure it was.

He led her to the sofa. "Curl up here. I'll come get you when your bath is ready."

She must have dozed off because she startled and yelped when she felt herself being lifted into the air.

"Easy, Sunshine. I've got you."

"I can walk." But this was nice, too. She burrowed her face against his neck, his familiar spicy scent soothing her.

"I'm sure you can." When he reached the bathroom, he set her on a granite counter that was longer than her kitchen. "Your overnight bag is here, but since I don't know what Taylor packed for you, here's one of my T-shirts if you need it. If you'd rather have a robe, there's one hanging on the back of the door."

She glanced over to see a long-sleeve tee on top of her tote. "Thanks."

"I don't have any bath oils or salts to add to it, which I will correct ASAP, but the water's nice and warm. Take as long as you need. I'm going to make you something to eat before I tuck you into bed. Call me if you need any help washing your hair or whatever."

He kissed her nose and then left her alone. "You're a keeper, Rand Stevens," she whispered. She shucked her clothes, then sighed as she eased her body into the water. The oversize tub was a Jacuzzi, and he'd turned the jets on low. God, that felt good.

After Taylor had left her in Nate's office, Kinsey had refused to think of Sebastian spying on her, and she continued to block him from her mind. She'd deal with it when she felt better. Music came on, playing softly. She lifted her gaze to the ceiling to see four speakers. The music was instrumental, and she leaned her head back, closed her eyes, and did nothing but listen to the soft sounds of the orchestra.

When the water began to cool, she pulled the plug, then hopped over to a shower that could easily hold six people and washed her hair. By the time she dried off with a soft, thick towel, she felt better. And clean, which seemed a miracle in itself.

She dug her toiletries and hairbrush from her overnight bag. Taylor had packed a pair of jeans, two T-shirts, undies, and two pairs of yoga pants. Kinsey slipped on panties, the yoga pants, and Rand's T-shirt. It came to almost her knees and she had to roll the sleeves up, and although it didn't make sense, she felt safe wearing it. An illusion, but right now she'd take anything she could get to keep the turmoil trying to sneak into her mind at bay.

Barefoot, she padded into the kitchen. "Something smells really good." Rand glanced over his shoulder and smiled, and her toes curled in response. Maybe she wasn't dead inside after all.

"Homemade chicken noodle soup. It's good for the soul

and heals all that ails you, or so grandmothers around the world claim."

Then give her a ton of it. "Homemade by?"

"Me." He gestured to the island where two places were set with bowls, bread plates, and two glasses of water with lemon slices floating on the top. "Pull out a stool and sit."

"You cook?" She'd imagined that... Well, she really didn't know what she thought of his private life. Things had happened so fast between them that there was still so much she didn't know about him. Did that mean she didn't really love him, had only gotten caught up in the idea of loving him?

"Stop thinking, Sunshine. There'll be plenty of time for that later. To answer your question, I cook soups. Egg things like omelets or scrambled. And I can make a mean sandwich. That's about it."

He set a large white bowl with a lid on it on the island, then took a loaf of bread from the oven and sliced it. She hadn't thought she was hungry, but the aromas of fresh-baked bread and soup had her mouth watering.

"Sourdough bread straight from San Francisco," he said, sliding the platter of bread onto the counter. "Butter up while it's hot."

"Who gets sourdough straight from San Fran?" she said before she thought better of it.

His gaze flew to hers. "I do. If you haven't already figured it out, I'm rich. It wasn't my doing, so I can't claim to be a rags-to-riches story like my father can. Sure, it's nice to have that kind of money, but it doesn't define my life. Things have progressed pretty fast for us"—she nodded in agreement—"so maybe this is a good time to tell you about the man you're in love with."

If she really was. She believed she was, but today she was doubting everything she thought she knew. "Yes, please tell me about you." Not only did she want to know him, but his voice was another thing that soothed her, and she wondered if he'd talk all night long if she asked.

He told her about his parents, he told her how he'd been inspired to apply to the FBI because of a boy named Tyrone. He talked about his marriage again and how much he missed his little girl, but that he finally knew he was capable of loving again, something he'd believed had been lost to him forever.

Then he started talking about her, how the minute she'd walked into Aces & Eights, he couldn't stop thinking about her. "You brought the sunshine back into my life, Kinsey. I love you, and we'll get through this together."

She lowered her gaze to her bowl, wanting to hide her tears from him. Everything he'd said had deeply touched her. What a joke to even question if she loved this beautiful man.

"I was wondering earlier if I really did love you or if I'd gotten caught up in a moment," she said, deciding to be truthful with him. She frowned. "My bowl is full again."

He smirked. "For the third time. And you do love me, so stop trying to analyze something that just is."

"You did that on purpose, talked my ear off so I'd eat."

"Busted. Now let's get you to bed."

"I'll help you clean up."

"No, you won't." He held out his hand.

"I feel like such a baby." She put her hand in his and walked with him to the bedroom. "Will you stay with me?"

"Climb in. I need to make a phone call and put the soup away. I'll be back soon. It's been a long time since I've taken an afternoon nap, especially with a gorgeous woman in my bed."

After he left, she pulled off her yoga pants and slipped into probably the biggest, softest bed in the world. She'd thought she would fall instantly to sleep, but every time she closed her eyes, she saw Sebastian's face. Soft music still played from the speakers, so she shut her mind to all but the piano concerto.

Rand returned a few minutes later, shucked his jeans, shoes, and socks, then slid into the bed. When he spooned her and wrapped an arm around her waist, she sighed from the pleasure of having him pressed against her.

"Are you too sleepy to talk for a few minutes?" he asked.

"I don't know if I can sleep. When I close my eyes, I see his face."

"That's what I want to talk about." He reached for her hand and laced his fingers around hers. "You did nothing wrong, Kinsey. You're not to blame for what he did."

"I know that, and that's not what bothers me."

"Then tell me what does."

She was glad she faced away from him because it made it easier to talk about it. "He watched me, Rand. Watched me undress, take a bath. God, did he even watch me pee?" His hand tightened around hers, but he didn't speak, which she appreciated. "He made me feel dirty. And part of it is my fault. I didn't take his harassment seriously, and I should have. If I had, I would have reported him, even if it meant losing my job."

"First, you're not dirty, Sunshine. Not even close." He tightened his hold on her. "This is all on him. I know that's easy for me to say, but think about this. If you let him put that thought in your head, you're letting him win."

"Yeah, but getting my mind to believe that isn't so easy."

"Finding out you were being watched isn't a small thing. It's not like some jerk giving you a wolf whistle as you walk by that you can ignore. He violated you in one of the worst ways possible. Give yourself a little time to get your head straight and accept that you aren't responsible in any way for his actions. It also might help to talk to someone, a professional who deals in sexual assaults."

"Maybe." She turned and faced him. "Since you've brought that up, I've been thinking. Have you ever considered doing that? You know, talking to someone who specializes in coping with loss?" She had been wanting to talk to him about seeing a therapist, and he'd just given her the opening to bring it up.

After hesitating, he said, "Honestly, before meeting you, I didn't want to feel better. It seemed like it would be a betrayal to my daughter if I ever let go of the pain that lived in my heart. That how deeply I hurt was proof of how much I loved and missed her."

She rested her palm on his face. "Oh, Rand, that's—"

"Not true. I know that now. And maybe it is time to talk to someone. We'll discuss this some more, but right now you need to get some rest."

"Yeah, I am tired. Tomorrow I need to start looking for a job since there's no way I can go back to Summer Fashions."

Rand wanted to tell her that she didn't need the job, that he would take care of her. Since he doubted that would go over well, he kept that to himself. "Did you like working there?"

"Yeah, except for Sebastian. I doubt Mr. Summer will give me a good reference."

"Yes, he will. Trust me on that." He'd make sure of it.

"I hope so. I not only lost my job but my apartment, too. I feel like he stole everything from me."

"Move in with me." He held his breath, waiting for her answer.

"It's too soon to take that step."

"No, it isn't. What I feel for you is real. If not for what happened, we wouldn't be talking about this yet, but I don't for a minute doubt that I want us to make a life together."

"I could move in with one of my brothers."

"Is that what you really want to do?" He wouldn't be happy about that, but he'd support her if that was what she decided.

"Not really. I mean, I love them and their families, but they're a little overbearing."

He chuckled. "And overwhelming."

"That, too. Are you sure you want me to live with you?"

"I've never been more sure of anything, Sunshine. I love you."

"And I love you, too. But let's call it a trial period for a month. If it doesn't feel like it's working for either one of us, I'll find another place."

He'd make it work however he had to. "Now that we have that settled, we're going to stop talking so you can go to sleep." He put his hand on her face, spreading his fingers over her cheek. "But first, I need a kiss." Ah, there was a smile.

"Do you now?"

"More than anything." He brushed his lips across hers, then molded his mouth over hers. Being this close to her, having her body against his was killing him. He wanted her like crazy, but she needed to rest so she could heal. To keep her from feeling what she was doing to him, he shifted his lower body away from hers.

"Oscar," she said when he let go of her mouth.

He blinked. "Ah, Oscar?"

"Yes, the bird. He's a macaw, and he depends on me to feed him. I ran an ad in the paper but didn't include his name. Five people called claiming him, but couldn't tell me what he calls himself, so I guess he's mine."

The amount of relief that Oscar was a feathered male was ridiculous. Rand grinned. He was a goner, no doubt about it, and he was damn happy about it.

"Then we'll just have to move him in with us."

Her eyes lit up. "That's really okay with you?"

"If it means having you here, absolutely. Now go to sleep, my sunshine girl."

❧

Turned out that luring Oscar into a cage wasn't all that easy, but after three days of hopping around the cage, his beady eyes on the food inside, he finally went in.

"Bad boy!" Oscar screamed when Kinsey closed the door behind him.

"It's for your own good, Oscar." Kinsey looked up at Rand. "He's a little skinnier and more raggedy than he was the last time I saw him."

Rand eyed the screeching bird. "Is he always going to be that loud?" He might have to turn his third bedroom into a soundproof bird sanctuary.

She squatted next to the cage. "I don't think so. He just needs to settle down. We'll buy him some toys and whatever else a bird needs to be happy."

He laughed. "Of course we will."

"You are going to be happier, Oscar. I promise." She stuck a finger past the bars and scratched his neck.

"Well, I guess that's it, we're done here?" He glanced around. They'd already moved all the things she wanted to keep to his place, mostly her clothes and personal belongings. Her furniture she'd donated to a charity. All that had been left was Oscar, and they'd come each afternoon to her apartment, attempting to catch her bird.

"Yep." She looked up at him, a soft smile on her face. "It's a new day and a new life from here on out."

"Come here." He held out his arms. With happiness shining in her eyes, she walked into his embrace. "I love you, Sunshine, but I reserve judgment on loving that mangy thing you're bringing with you."

"He'll win you over." She chewed on her bottom lip as she glanced at Oscar, still expressing his displeasure at being caged. "I think."

"Doesn't matter as long as I have you." He sealed that pledge with a kiss.

They'd made love last night for only the second time since meeting each other, and it had been intense and beautiful. He'd never expected to fall in love again, to even want to, and their romance had been unusual to say the least. In the back of his mind he worried they'd reached this point too fast. Not for him. He didn't have any doubts about how he felt about her. He loved her with a fierceness that surprised him.

It was her he worried about. Had it happened too fast for her, and had the circumstances played too big of a role? He knew he made her feel protected, but when she felt safe again, would she realize that it wasn't love she was experiencing? He'd ask her to marry him right now, this minute, if he was sure her love for him was real. That was how certain he was that she was the one.

"Ready to go?"

"I am." He gave her one more quick kiss, then picked up the cage.

"Oscar's a bad boy!"

Rand glanced at the bird. "He sure as hell is."

"Hell," Oscar squawked.

CHAPTER SIXTEEN

KINSEY LIFTED HER FACE TO the morning sun. "This is nice." She lazily rolled her head toward Aiden. "I've missed you." Since being drafted, his time seemed to be owned by the Dolphins.

They were stretched out on lounge chairs on the roof of Rand's building. Surrounded by tall, lush potted plants, it was a garden paradise. A place she liked starting her day while she drank her morning coffee. Rand usually joined her before heading off to work, but he'd declined to come up with her today, saying she needed some alone time with her friend. She smiled, thinking it was a rare man who wouldn't have a problem with his girl being close friends with a star football player and one as good-looking as Aiden. Her guy was amazing.

"Right back at you, kiddo." She'd made mimosas for them, and he took a sip of his. "This is good, but only one for me. Got a long day of practice ahead." He glanced over at her. "Every time I think of what that man did to you, I want to kill him."

She rolled her eyes. "I never realized before how blood-thirsty men were. You'll have to get in line behind Rand and my brothers."

"Make sure they know to include me if they ever decide to teach him a lesson." He shook his head. "I'm still trying to wrap my mind around you all of a sudden having brothers. Add to that they're all FBI, and then add to that you've gone and fallen in love with an FBI agent"—he swept his arm out—"and let's not forget a rich one with a roof garden on top of his penthouse apartment…" He started laughing. "You have to admit that's all hard to take in."

She snorted. "Tell me about it."

"Are you happy, Kinsey?"

"Yeah, I am. More than I ever thought possible."

"That's all that counts then."

Yes, it really was.

After Aiden left, she showered and dressed for the job interview scheduled for late morning. It was a second interview, and she was excited. Her position at Summer Fashions had been as a junior buyer, and this one was for a full-fledged buyer for Cheeky Chic, an upscale chain of women's boutiques.

Her phone rang as she was drying her hair, and she frowned at seeing Corrie's name on the screen. Kinsey wasn't sure she wanted to talk to the woman who'd advised her that the way to handle Sebastian was to just ignore him. Still, she was curious, so she answered.

"Hello."

"Kinsey, this is Corrie. I wanted to tell you how sorry I am for what happened to you. I swear I had no idea Sebastian would do something like that."

"Did you know about the others?" That was the one question she wanted an answer to. If Corrie had known, then she should have realized what Sebastian was capable of. And if she had known, Kinsey wasn't sure she could forgive her saying Sebastian was harmless when she knew he wasn't.

"No, not the details of what he did. Not until all this came out after he was arrested. I did know something happened with one of the women, but when she didn't show up for work one day, Mr. Summer said that she'd made false accusations in an attempt to extort money. I wasn't working there when the incidents before her happened."

Kinsey thought Corrie probably did know more than

she was admitting to, and she hoped her former boss had learned a lesson. "All I have to say is that if another of your employees finds herself being sexually harassed, I hope you'll do more than advise her to ignore it."

There was a moment of silence, then, "I should have done more for you. I know it, and I'm truly sorry, Kinsey. Please believe that. The other thing I wanted to tell you is that I resigned. Not that you care or even should, but it was my own protest to what happened to you."

"Hm, okay." She really wasn't sure what to say. Mr. Summer had thought very highly of his head buyer, and there was a bit of satisfaction in hearing that he'd lost his favorite employee because of what his son did.

"Before I left, I took a call from the HR director for Cheeky Chic, asking for a reference. I told him that you were one of the most talented buyers I'd ever worked with, and that if they didn't hire you, they were stupid."

"Thanks, I appreciate that."

"I didn't say anything that wasn't true. Kinsey, I wish you the best." She disconnected.

Kinsey stared at her phone for a moment before setting it back on the counter, not sure how she felt about the call. If nothing else, it was a closure between her and Corrie. One thing she promised herself was that if she was ever in the position Corrie had been in, she wouldn't turn a blind eye.

☾

Rand stood at the bar of Aces & Eights, surveying the crowd. It was one of those nights. They'd broken up three fights already and had banned the Tricksters Motor Club for a month for bringing weapons into the bar.

"Not liking tonight much," Spider said, coming to stand next to him.

"Tell me about it." But it was Rand's last night at Aces & Eights, so that was the good news.

Nate had found his replacement, who was here tonight getting the lay of the land. The dude… Rand gave a mental shake of his head. The *man* was biker bad boy right down to the chains hanging out of his pockets and the tattoo sleeves decorating both arms. No one would peg him as an undercover FBI agent. Josh was already enamored of the man and would be in good hands with his new dude friend.

Josh had finally gotten the Hot Shots to trust him, so that investigation was heating up. Rand was relieved that he wouldn't be a part of it. He went to the office to box up the few personal belongings he had here. He wondered if he'd miss the bar. He thought about it for a moment. "Nah." It was doubtful that anyone would even notice he was gone. Spider, maybe, but that was about it.

It was Friday night, and Monday he'd be back in the field where he belonged. A month had passed since Kinsey and her noisy bird had moved in, meaning their… not their, *her* trial period of living together was up. He had big plans for tomorrow night.

He texted Josh, letting him know that he was leaving, then picked up his one box and headed for the door. Before he got to it, Josh came barreling in.

"Dude, tell me you weren't going to leave without saying goodbye." He tackled Rand in a bear hug.

"Josh, I'm not disappearing from your life, you know." He gave his fellow agent an awkward pat on the back. "You can let go of me now."

"Gonna miss those sour looks on your ugly mug when the bikers come in the door."

After extricating himself from Josh's hold, he said, "Nah, you've got a new partner to break in. You won't even think about me."

A wide grin appeared on Josh's face. "He is one cool dude." He held out his arms. "I'm thinking I need some tattoos."

"No, you don't." He squeezed Josh's shoulder. "You watch your back when you're at the bar, you hear?"

Surprisingly he did feel a trace of regret as he walked out of the door of Aces & Eights for the last time.

𝕮

It was Saturday night, and Rand was taking Kinsey out to dinner on the pretense of celebrating her new position as the buyer at Cheeky Chic.

One of the many things they'd found they had in common was the love of trying new foods. She'd never eaten in an authentic French restaurant, so he was taking her to the best one Miami had to offer.

"Mr. Stevens, we have your table ready," the maître d' said at seeing him.

Rand saw the surprise on Kinsey's face that Marc recognized him on sight, but he just smiled. "Thank you, Marc." He slid his palm down to Kinsey's lower back. "My lady is looking forward to enjoying Gregory's selections." Rand would almost consider marrying Gregory Pugin if they played on the same team. His food was that good.

Marc smiled at Kinsey. "You're in for a treat, *mademoiselle*. Please follow me."

They were led to the table that Rand had requested, one set in the back, giving him and Kinsey privacy. "Will you be ordering from the menu or the chef's selections tonight, Mr. Stevens?" Marc asked after they were seated.

"Are you good with the six-course chef's selection?" he asked Kinsey. "That will give you a little taste of everything. Or you can order from the menu."

She turned those sexy-as-hell smoky eyes on him. "I'm at your mercy tonight. You promised to teach me new things."

Rand's brain short-circuited, getting stuck on all the ways he could answer those two sentences.

"You will enjoy the chef's creations then," Marc said to

Kinsey before turning to Rand. "It is good to see you out again, Mr. Stevens, especially with such a beautiful lady. Do you wish to choose the wine or go with the chef's wine pairings?"

"Ah, right, the wine." He gave himself a mental shake, glad that the tablecloth hid him below the belt. "Kinsey? Marceau's has an extensive wine collection, and Marc will bring you the wine menu if you wish. However, I recommend you allow the chef to choose the wine to go with each of your selections."

"That would be fun."

"The wine pairings for the lady, and I'll have a club soda on ice with a lime."

Marc nodded. "Your waiter tonight is Brandon. I'll give him your selections."

After Marc left, Rand glanced around, then turned his gaze on Kinsey. "You know what I don't see?"

"What's that?"

"I can't find another woman here tonight as beautiful as you. Don't be obvious, but see the man two tables to my right?" At her nod, he said, "He's sneaking peeks at you. He wishes he were me."

She lowered her lashes as she smiled, and that shy smile touched something deep inside Rand. Before her, he'd been used to women who knew they were gorgeous, whose smiles were artificial, and who accepted compliments as their due. Kinsey was real, nothing practiced about her, and her honesty shone in her eyes. She owned his heart. He slipped his hand into his suit coat and fingered the two items in it. They felt warm on his skin, as if confirming what he planned for tonight was right.

"I love you, my sunshine girl," he said, getting her eyes back on him. "Yesterday our trial date of living together was up, and you're still here. Are you going to stay? Just so you know, your answer determines whether I ever breathe again."

She slid her hand across the table, palm up. "Take my hand."

He placed his over hers, and as always happened when he touched her, he felt something powerful pass between them.

When their fingers were linked, she said, "It amazes me how easily I do breathe when you're near. You're my rock, my soul mate, and damn awesome in bed. I'm staying."

He choked on a laugh. "I never know whether to laugh or cry around you, Kins. Promise you'll always keep me on my toes."

"My life's mission. How fast can we eat?"

"There you go, leaving me in the dust. Why?"

"I'm feeling awfully needy." She winked. "You know, the kind that requires special attention from her man."

Leave it to her to mess with his mind. He had plans for tonight. On the other hand, he could eat pretty damn fast if she was waiting at the finish line.

Before he could answer, Brandon arrived, setting a plate between them. "For your first course, the chef has selected *Le Caviar D'Oscietra*. Quail eggs with oscietra caviar, cauliflower puree, and baby gem lettuce. *Bon appetite.*"

Rand put one of the items from his pocket in the hand Brandon held below the table. He'd arranged this, and as much as he wanted to scoop Kinsey up and carry her home so he could give her that special attention, he was determined that the night would proceed as planned.

The sommelier arrived right behind with Kinsey's first course wine pairing. "For the lady, an Erpacrife Nebbiolo, the perfect complement to the salty flavor of the sea."

"It's too bad you don't drink," Kinsey said after tasting the wine. "This is superb."

"Take another sip." After she did, he leaned across the table. "Come here." When her face was inches from his, he kissed her. Once his mouth was on hers, he had to remind himself they were surrounded by other diners. He sat back, very much liking how her eyes had turned darker with nothing more than the brush of their lips against each other.

"You're right. The wine is superb." And so was her mouth.

By the time they reached dessert, Rand didn't think he could eat another bite. But he was pretty sure Kinsey would like the crepes Suzette he'd requested. Even more, he prayed she loved the champagne that came with it.

The crepes were prepared tableside, which seemed to fascinate her. When Brandon lit the alcohol to flambé the crepes, she clapped in delight, which sent such a warm feeling to Rand's heart that he wasn't sure he could wait until her glass of champagne arrived to ask his question. But he had a plan, and damn if he'd mess it up with his eagerness to take them to the next step in their relationship.

"Oh my God, these are good." She closed her eyes and moaned when she put a second bite in her mouth.

"Kinsey," he growled. "If you don't stop making those noises, I'm going to have you right here on this table and embarrass us both in front of everyone."

The little minx moaned again. She'd be lucky if they made it to his car before he was on her.

"Mr. Stevens specifically requested our best champagne for his lady," Brandon said, placing a cut crystal wineglass in front of her. "Drink it slowly, *mademoiselle*, as there are treasures to be found within."

Marc had balked when Rand had called him a few days ago to arrange tonight, worried that Kinsey would swallow the surprise in the glass. Rand had promised he wouldn't let that happen.

"That was an odd thing to say," she said after the waiter left. As she brought the glass to her lips, she glanced down at it and stilled. Then her gaze shot up to his. "Maybe not so odd."

With his heart pounding, he watched her fish the ring

out. He knew he might be pushing things too fast, but he wanted his ring on her finger, even if she wanted to hold off on a wedding for a while.

"Rand," she whispered.

He took the ring from her and held it between them. "Because of you, I'm smiling again. Because of you, I look forward to each new day again. Because of you, my heart beats again. I love you, Kinsey, with all that I am. Will you marry me?"

"Yes," she said as tears pooled in her eyes. "Oh yes."

"Give me your hand." He slipped the ring onto her finger.

She held her hand up to the light. "It's beautiful."

"You're beautiful." He knew she wouldn't have wanted anything showy, and he'd found what he thought was the perfect ring for her, a simple platinum band with a flawless two-carat cushion-cut diamond. Okay, it was a little showy, but out of all the ones he'd looked at, it was the one that called to him.

"Did I remember to tell you that I love you?"

She stared up as she tapped her finger on her lips, flashing the diamond at him. "Hmm, let me think." She lowered her gaze to him. "I'm not sure. Maybe you should tell me again."

He took her hand and brushed his thumb over the ring, liking it on her finger even more than he thought he would. "I love you, Sunshine, so much it hurts to breathe sometimes. There's one other thing I want to give you." He removed Zoe's necklace from his pocket. "I told you about this necklace. I've carried it with me every day since Zoe died. I want you to keep it safe until we can give it to our daughter."

"Oh, Rand." She took the necklace from him, then lifted tear-filled eyes to his. "And we'll tell our daughter all about her sister."

"I didn't mean to make you cry." He reached across the

table and swiped his thumb over her cheek, even as he blinked his own tears away. "This is a special night, not one to be sad, okay?"

"I'm not. Honest." She smiled. "But I am deeply touched."

"That's okay then." Before they both started crying, he lifted a hand to signal for the check.

"Let's go home. I have a need to make love to my fiancée."

☾

"Come here, Sunshine."

Kinsey gently placed Zoe's necklace into her jewelry box before glancing over her shoulder at Rand. "Why? You have something in mind?" Her man was mouthwateringly sexy sitting on the edge of their bed, his gaze hot and heavy on her.

"You know I do."

She kicked off her shoes before walking to him and stopping between his legs. "Have you seen my gorgeous ring that someone gave me tonight?" She dangled her fingers in front of his face.

"Just someone?"

"Well, he is a very special someone."

He took her hand, brought it to his lips, and placed a kiss on the center of her palm. Then he pulled her onto his lap and lowered his mouth to hers.

The kiss was gentle... slow, as if he had all the time in the world. His lips were warm and soft, and the feel of his thumb as he made circles, caressing the skin below her ear, sent delicious shivers through her. She sighed into his mouth, and he answered with a groan. He lifted his head and stared at her for a moment, and the need in his eyes made her heart flutter. She splayed her hand over his chest. He put his hand over hers, and then his mouth found hers again.

It wasn't a gentle kiss this time. He took possession,

claimed her as his. His tongue was a magical thing. He teased her and tasted her, and it seemed as if he couldn't get enough. She was riding the edge and he hadn't even touched her anywhere but her mouth, her neck, and her hand.

"Rand," she whispered against his lips, a plea for more.

He pulled away and rested his forehead against hers. "Do we have a fire extinguisher nearby?"

"Hmm?" They were both breathing heavily, and he'd obviously stolen her ability to think because she couldn't make sense of his question.

"We might ignite when we get to the good part."

Ah, that. "Maybe, but I'm willing to risk it."

He chuckled. "Adventurous. I like it. But we have on too many clothes."

"I know you do." He'd removed his suit coat and tie when they'd gotten home, but that still left his pants and shirt.

"Let me." She brushed his fingers away from his buttons. As she undressed him, he kept his eyes on hers, and there was so much love in them for her that her heart felt like it was melting. Once she had his shirt off, he put his hands on her knees. He slid the hem of her dress up, letting his fingers trail a sensual line up her inner thighs.

"I'm taking over now," he said as he pulled her dress over her head.

After their clothes were in a pile on the floor, he pulled her onto the bed with him. He stared up at her, the heat in his eyes searing her right down to her core, leaving her with a gooey center and an ache between her thighs.

Sprawled over him, she cupped his face with her palms and brushed her lips over his. "I love you," she whispered against his mouth.

A rumbling growl sounded from deep in his throat as he flipped them over. "I'm going to love you all night long, Sunshine. Slow and easy later, but right now I'm feeling a little out of control, so hang on tight."

"I like you out of control."

He barked a laugh. "Then you're about to like me a whole lot." He kissed her hard, his tongue tasting every inch of her mouth. From there he moved to her neck, sucking hard enough to mark her. He'd never done that before, never put his claim on her. But tonight it was exactly what she wanted, and she had every intention of putting her mark on him before the night was over.

He took her mouth in a scorching kiss while his fingers found their way to her sex. He played her like a maestro strumming his beloved instrument. By the time he entered her, he'd tasted every part of her body, letting her climax twice but only after she'd begged.

"My sunshine," he softly said when he was buried to the hilt.

It was the first time they were making love without a condom, and the feel of him was amazing. She wrapped her legs around his, slid her hands down to his butt, turned her head, and sank her teeth into his upper arm.

"Sweet Jesus, Kins." He shuddered as he thrust into her. "I didn't know it would feel this damn good not to have anything between us." As he'd promised, he loved her hard and fast, and just when she was ready to leap off the edge, he said, "Now, babe. Take me with you."

She squeezed hard, wrapping her core muscles around him until he felt nothing but her.

"Damn," he gasped. He held on to her as if he'd never let her go as they soared together. "Damn," he softly said again. After they'd floated back down to earth, their mingling breaths still heavy and harsh, he nuzzled his face into her neck.

"We've only just begun, Kinsey," he whispered into her ear.

"I might die." She found his hand and laced their fingers together. "Did it feel good, you know, to be bare inside me?"

"I don't even have the words for how good it felt."

After moving in together, they'd both gone to the doctor and gotten a clean bill of health, and she'd already been on the pill. Even so, he'd refused to make love to her without a condom, and she'd assumed he wanted the double protection against a pregnancy. Now she realized he was saving their first time without having anything between them for tonight. How long had he been planning his proposal?

"Don't think I can move," he muttered.

She rubbed her cheek on his. "Ah, so that 'I'm going to love you all night long' was just big talk?"

"Hush, woman. I keep my promises."

Several hours later, sated and boneless, she listened to Rand's even breaths. Too keyed up to sleep, she eased out from under his arm and slid out of bed. In the living room she turned on a lamp, dimming it to low, then curled up in the corner of the sofa. She held up her hand and admired her ring. "Look, Mom, I'm engaged!"

What a crazy few months it had been. Not only finding her brothers but actually liking them. It still boggled the mind that they were FBI, and that she was going to marry an FBI agent. In a million years she never would have guessed that. She and Rand were both seeing a therapist, and it was already easier for him to talk about having kids someday. He no longer broke out in a sweat. The only thing she was sad about now was that her mother and Zoe weren't here to see her and Rand get married.

"I miss you so much, Mom. In your letter you said you only asked that I be happy. Well, I want you to know that I am, more than I thought I'd ever be. I found my brothers, and they're amazing. You'd be so proud of them. And guess what? I'm getting married to the most wonderful man. I wish you could have met him, Mom. You would have loved him. I hope you can hear me, because I have a special favor to ask. Do you think you can find a little girl named

Zoe and take care of her for Rand?"

In her heart she believed her mother could hear her. She hoped so. After wiping away her tears, she went back to bed. As she snuggled up to Rand, he mumbled nonsense words while wrapping his body around hers, cocooning her in the safety of his arms.

The last thing she thought of before falling asleep was the matching hickey he sported on his neck. She smiled, knowing her brothers were going to razz him to no end when seeing it. Well, unless they killed him for marking her. A giggle escaped at the thought of her brothers messing with Rand, which they loved to do.

"Sumpin' funny?" he muttered, more asleep than awake.

"Not a thing, babe." She grinned, fully aware she'd just fibbed.

CHAPTER SEVENTEEN

"DUDE," ALEX SAID, HIS GAZE narrowed on Rand's neck. "Tell me a bee stung you and you didn't have my sister doing dirty things to you."

"*Dude*, none of your business." Rand knew he'd get shit from the Gentrys at the Saturday afternoon cookout that had become a tradition since Kinsey and her brothers had discovered each other. He could have worn a shirt with a collar instead of a tee, but he was damn proud of Kinsey's mark on him and had no intention of hiding it.

"He said 'dude,' dudes," Alex said, his gaze going from Court to Nate. "Does that mean he's finally one of us?"

Court lifted one shoulder in a half-hearted shrug. "He's getting there."

"We'll bring him to the dark side eventually," Nate said with a smirk on his face. Then he leveled a hard gaze on Rand. "Not sure why, but you seem to make her happy. As long as she has a smile on her face, you get to live."

"Good to know," Rand muttered.

Nate's expression turned serious. "I've got some news. A trial date has been set for Summer for next month. His attorney asked for a plea bargain, but the DA refused. The evidence against him is strong enough that the DA's confident he'll get the maximum."

"That's great news." Apparently tired of getting his son out of trouble, Jacob Summer hadn't posted his bail. Rand wished Kinsey's involvement with the man was done. "I thought Kinsey might be dreading the trial, but when she learned of his past deeds, she said she couldn't wait to get on the witness stand and do her part in sending him to prison." He was damn proud of her.

"Good for her," Court said.

A bloodcurdling shriek had him and the brothers reaching for their guns.

"Oh my God, Kinsey," Madison screamed. "What's that on your hand? It's blinding my eyes."

"A ring?" Alex said.

"Yep." Rand smiled when Kinsey waved her hand in front of the Gentry wives.

"Thought it would take a little longer but not surprised," Court said.

"When I know what I want, I don't waste time."

Alex scowled. "Dude, you're supposed to ask us for permission to marry her."

"Oops."

Nate held up his beer. "Congratulations. But if you ever make her cry, I'll shoot you."

"Tough crowd," Rand said.

"The toughest," Nate agreed.

"Well, this calls for a celebration." Alex stood. "I've got some champagne Madison and I bought last New Year's but never got around to drinking. Her fault. She distracted me when she—"

"TMI, baby brother." Court reached into the cooler and grabbed a handful of ice, throwing the cubes at Alex's retreating back.

"Dude, you'll pay for that," Alex called over his shoulder.

"If he teaches my kids to say 'dude,' I'll never forgive him," Rand said.

Nate narrowed his eyes. "She's not pregnant, is she?"

"Not yet." But he was looking forward to the day she was, and wasn't that something? "We're talking about a destination wedding. Some island, maybe St. Thomas. Just our families, and the expense is on me for everyone. Wherever we decide on, I'll charter a plane so we won't have to deal with a gaggle of children on a commercial flight."

"I might like having you for a brother-in-law after all," Nate said.

Rand grinned. "Thought you'd say that."

☾

The St. Thomas weather was picture-perfect. Sunset was two hours away, only two more hours before Kinsey would be his wife. Rand couldn't wait. But he had something to do first. He slipped away from his soon-to-be brothers-in-law for a few minutes of quiet time. There was a cove a little ways from the resort, and he made his way to it. A grouping of palm trees stood tall near the water, their fronds swaying in the breeze. He stopped in their shade and looked out over the turquoise waters of the Caribbean Sea.

"You'd love it here, Zoe," he said. "I'm beginning a new life. Maybe you already know that, and if so, I hope that makes you happy. After I lost you, I thought I'd never smile again, but then Kinsey came along. She taught me that being happy again doesn't mean I love you any less. You would have loved her, your new aunts and uncles, and your cousins. They're very noisy, though." He chuckled. She would have been delighted by the chaos of life among the Gentrys. "I came to this spot where it's just you and me to make you a promise. I'll never forget you, baby girl. You will always live on in my heart."

He squeezed his burning eyes closed and pinched the bridge of his nose. "I love you, Zoe," he whispered. The melodious sound of a child's laughter—so much like Zoe's—reached his ears, and he shuddered. There had to be someone with a little girl nearby, but he walked away without looking for her, choosing to believe that Zoe had found a way to let him know she was in a good place and that she was happy for him.

When he reached the beach in front of the resort, three tall males stood on the sand, arms crossed over their chests, watching him.

He stopped in front of them. "If some kind of initiation into the family is about to happen, all I ask is that you don't make me bleed. That won't look pretty in our wedding photos."

"Saw you sneaking off. Just making sure you weren't running away, dude," Alex said.

Court dangled handcuffs in front of Rand. "One way or another, our sister is getting married today."

"Ignore these two clowns," Nate said. He glanced over at the cove. "You good now?"

"Yeah. I am." The Gentry brothers never missed a trick, and he should have known there was no sneaking away from them. They'd also guessed he needed a moment with his daughter and had given it to him but were letting him know they were here for him. He nodded. "Real good, in fact."

"Then let's go get you married."

🝔

Rand stood at the water's edge under a sky painted in shades of pinks and yellows by the setting sun. He and his best men—all three Gentry brothers—wore tuxes and were barefoot. He'd thought he might be nervous, but the only emotion he felt was impatience to hear the words pronouncing him and Kinsey husband and wife.

He glanced at the only family members not in the wedding party. Rosie held Max, Court and Lauren's baby, and Alex and Madison's son, Michael, sat between her and Rand's father. At the moment Harlan was showing something on his phone to Michael, probably pictures of fire trucks, the boy's obsession. Rand's mother looked on with faint amusement. She'd warmed up to the Gentrys some, which was impressive in itself.

Giggles preceded the flower girls. He grinned at seeing six barefoot little girls dropping rose petals on the sand as they walked toward him. Each wore a different colored pastel sundress, making him think of a rainbow. To prevent a mutiny, Kinsey had sealed her status as favorite new aunt by asking all six of Taylor and Nate's daughters to be her flower girls. Well, five of them were dropping petals. Annie was picking them up and putting them in her basket.

"No, Annie," Bri said. "The bride has to walk on them so her feet will smell pretty."

"Nothing worse than a bride with stinky feet," Alex murmured, making his brothers snort and Rand outright laugh.

Bri managed to get Annie to drop her petals, and when they reached Rand, they surprised him by curtseying. He gave them a formal bow, which made them giggle some more. The girls took the front-row seats that they'd been told were reserved for them. Well, except for Annie, who was tugging on Nate's pants, wanting to be picked up.

"Annie," Bri hissed. "You're supposed to sit with us."

"Don't want to." She lifted her arms up. "Hold me, Daddy."

Nate's eyes turned soft, something Rand only saw from him when he looked at one of his daughters or Taylor. Nate squatted and whispered something into Annie's ear, then kissed her nose. Whatever he said worked, and Annie joined her sisters.

The Gentry wives stepped out from the tent that had been set up by the wedding planner. Their ankle-length dresses were the same and had all the colors of the girls' dresses. Taylor, Lauren, and Madison held hands as they walked together toward him. Rand glanced at the brothers to see soft smiles on their faces as each looked at his own wife. The women took their places on the other side of him.

He was damn lucky, not only in finding and falling in

love with Kinsey, but in the family that came along with her. More than just his fellow agents, the brothers were now his family, too, and he couldn't have found more loyal and honorable men if he'd tried. And their wives were beautiful inside and out. He swallowed hard as it hit him just how fortunate he was.

The soft music that had been playing changed to the wedding march, and he turned his attention to the tent, his heart doing a dance in his chest as he waited to see his bride.

And there she is.

He exhaled a long breath. Beautiful didn't seem adequate. She wore a long, cream-colored silk slip dress that had thin straps. Her hair fell in soft waves over her shoulders, one side pinned up by the silver comb her mother had given her. She held an arrangement of tropical flowers, and in her ears were the diamond earrings that he'd given her as a wedding gift. Her only other jewelry was her engagement ring.

As Aiden escorted her to him, her eyes stayed locked on his, and a smile of happiness curved her lips. *Beautiful,* he mouthed. Her smile grew. She'd asked Aiden to walk with her because she said she couldn't pick just one brother to do it.

She stopped in front of him, and when he held out his hand, Aiden put her hand in his, then backed away and took a seat behind the girls. It was then that he noticed what her bouquet had been hiding. Wrapped around her wrist was Zoe's necklace. He'd thought his heart was already filled with love for this woman, but it miraculously expanded, making room for more.

"My sunshine," he whispered, then turned them to face the minister.

"Who is happy to see this woman be married to this man?"

"We are," her brothers said in unison.

Rand grinned. Kinsey had refused the traditional words of *who gives this woman*, saying that she wasn't anyone's to give away.

If asked later what was said between now and when he was told he could kiss his bride, he wouldn't have been able to answer. His heart, his mind, his very soul was filled with Kinsey, leaving no room for anything else. They'd been told this would happen, thus the video being filmed. He and Kinsey would watch their wedding video later tonight… among other things.

He did hear his permission to kiss his bride. He'd meant to make it a brief kiss, but kiss and brief where she was concerned was impossible.

"Dude, enough tonguing my sister," Alex muttered, making his brothers chuckle.

"Yuck, they're kissing," one of Nate's daughters exclaimed, causing every adult in attendance to laugh.

Rand pulled his mouth away from Kinsey's, then touched his forehead to hers. "How do we make them all go away?"

"Time for the last photo ops before the sun is gone," the photographer said.

He groaned.

C

Later that evening, after a delicious island-themed dinner with their families, Kinsey slipped her hand into her husband's as they walked onto the dance floor for the bride and groom dance. Their after-wedding party was taking place in a cordoned-off section of the resort's pool area. The ocean was visible, the moon full, the night magical.

"Mrs. Stevens, I believe this dance is mine," he said, stopping them in the middle of the floor. They'd only taken a few steps when he slid his hand to her wrist and wrapped his fingers around the necklace. "Thank you for this. You have no idea what it meant to me when I saw you wearing it. It felt like she was here with us."

"I think she was." The idea had come to her when she'd been going through her jewelry box, deciding what pieces to bring with her. She'd debated wearing it, then decided because of the sapphire stone in the heart, it would be her something blue. When she'd put it on her arm after getting dressed, she'd told her sisters-in-law the story behind it. With tears in their eyes, they'd each agreed it was a perfect way to honor Zoe's memory.

"If I told you that I have one more wedding present for you, what would you guess it was?"

She leaned her head back and looked up at him. "You already gave me a pair of gorgeous diamond earrings. That's more than enough."

"You're going to love this one even more. I'll give you a hint. It's something you once told me you've never done but wanted to."

After a moment of thinking, she said, "We're going to skydive?"

"Actually we are." He smiled at her. "I've made arrangements for us to do that this week. But that's not it. Guess again."

There was only one other thing she'd said the day he'd asked his question, and she gasped. "No way."

"Yes, way. We'll be attending the Paris Fashion Week."

"That is a very pleased-with-yourself smile on your face." And oh God, she was really going to the biggest fashion event in the world.

"I'll admit to that. Are you surprised?"

"Stunned might be a better word." She trailed the tips of her fingers across the back of his neck, thrilled when she felt him shiver. "I'll have to find a way to thank you later."

"I might have some ideas about that." He pulled her close and whispered in her ear. "How lucky am I to have the most beautiful bride in the history of the world? That dress is gorgeous on you, Sunshine, but I'm dying to take it off. When can we blow this joint?"

She laughed. "Patience, husband. They're all leaving in the morning. We'll have a whole week to ourselves. You can spend it taking off the clothes I put on."

He chuckled against her neck, sending shivers of pleasure down her back. "Trust me. I plan to keep you naked for the next seven days." He stepped back, spun her under his arm, then pulled her back to him. "And that's a promise, Mrs. Stevens. One of many I plan to keep."

"Kinsey Stevens," she said. "I love how that sounds." A year ago she'd been alone. Now she had a husband, brothers, sisters, nieces and nephews... a whole new amazing, wonderful life. In her deepest desires she'd never dared to wish for so much.

"What are you thinking?" her husband asked.

"That I'm blessed."

EPILOGUE

NATE GENTRY LEANED AGAINST THE entrance to his living room and smiled at seeing his brothers and Rand try to keep the children's attention off the pile of presents under the Christmas tree. At the moment Annie was attempting to sneak past Alex, her eyes glittering as bright as the shiny foil wrapping paper and sparkly bows.

"Oh no you don't, Annie girl," Alex said, snaking an arm around her little waist and then holding her up in the air, causing her to giggle.

Michael bounced on his feet as he lifted his arms up, wanting his daddy to hold him in the air, too. Max, Court and Lauren's son, was amusing himself by gumming his cousin Michael's toy fire truck.

"Where's Hemingway? Here, kitty, kitty," Oscar, Kinsey's bird, sang. Nate glanced over at the macaw that never seemed to stop talking. He was hopping around on top of his cage, stopping every few seconds to peer down at their cat. Hemingway sat on the arm of the sofa, his gaze fixated on Oscar. Hemingway meowed back at the bird. Oscar hopped down next to the cat, who immediately began to lick the bird, giving him a bath.

"Crazy animals," he muttered.

He looked down at the baby sleeping in his arms. He and Taylor had begun the process to adopt Elena. At three months she'd been left on the steps of the police station. Apparently being deaf made her unwanted. Taylor was learning sign language and teaching the rest of them so they'd all be able to communicate with her. He was impressed with how quickly the children were catching on to signing.

Elena opened her eyes and grinned at him, and Nate's heart melted as it did each time she favored him with a smile. She was such a happy baby, and he'd never understand how her mother could have abandoned her.

Although they'd agreed that six was their limit, he hadn't been able to say no to Taylor when she came home one day with Elena. She swore Elena was the last one. Nate hoped so, but he didn't quite believe her. If he didn't keep an eye on his wife, they'd run out of room and be house shopping again.

"Dude," Alex said, his back on the floor and children climbing on him. "You just going to stand there making goo-goo eyes at your daughter while these little monsters gang up on us?"

"Duuude," Michael yelled.

Nate laughed. *Dude* had been Michael's first word and remained his favorite one.

"Stop eating the fire truck, little man," Court said, picking up his son and then moving from the floor to the sofa. "The kid eats everything." He pulled a pacifier out of his shirt pocket and stuck it in Max's mouth.

The scene—him holding his seventh child, Alex covered up by a mob of giggling kids, Court carrying a pacifier around in his pocket—was so far from anything he'd ever thought possible that he wondered if it was real. Maybe he was having some kind of bizarre dream.

And then there was the sister they'd never known about. What a surprise that had been, but a good one. Kinsey was an amazing woman, and he and his brothers had gotten to know their mother again through her stories.

After some trial and error of trying to play protective big brothers and mostly getting it wrong, he and his brothers were learning to pick their battles where she was concerned. And he had to admit that if he'd been given the choice of picking her husband, it would have been Rand. But he didn't regret the hard time they'd given the man, even if Kinsey hadn't quite forgiven them for that. How else were they supposed to know for sure that Rand loved her and wouldn't hurt her? Rand got it and didn't hold it against them.

They'd add another member to the family in about two months when Rand and Kinsey's little boy was born. Nate thought it was probably good that their first child would be a boy, that it would be easier for Rand.

Rand grabbed Annie as she headed for the tree again. "This little girl has a one-track mind." He tickled her stomach, making her giggle.

The only one missing was Rosie. She'd recently announced that it was her turn to have some fun. The surprise, and it had been a big one, was that her new boyfriend was Spider. They'd hired him to do some work around the house, not abscond with their nanny, but the two were so ridiculously cute together that it was hard to be mad at Spider. And the children loved him, which wasn't surprising as he was as much a kid as they were. He and Rosie had decided to spend Christmas on a motorcycle trip to Key West. Nate shuddered at thinking of the two of them loose in the Keys.

"We're ready to feed the kids," Taylor said, coming to stand next to him.

Nate slipped an arm around her shoulders. "I was standing here thinking that if you'd told me a few years ago I'd have seven daughters, my brothers would marry and have kids, and that I'd find a long-lost sister, I would have laughed in your face."

"It's the seven daughters you're having trouble believing, isn't it?" She smiled up at him, laughter dancing in her beautiful blue eyes.

He glanced down at the baby cradled in his other arm.

"Yeah." He met his wife's gaze. "I still don't know if I deserve it, but I'm blessed."

"If anyone deserves to be blessed, Nate, it's you." She lifted onto her toes and kissed him. "Love you, babe. Gather up the kids and let's get them fed and to bed. Us ladies are wanting that romantic evening you guys promised us."

𝄢

"Alex, you set the table," Rand said. "Court, you can start grating the cheese for the scalloped potatoes. Nate, you're in charge of peeling the potatoes." He handed Nate a recipe that included a picture. "Slice them like this."

The deal they'd made with their wives was that if the girls got the kids fed and to bed, the guys would cook Christmas Eve dinner. They'd drawn straws, and Rand had picked the short one, making him head chef and meal planner.

It was quiet now compared to earlier in the evening, and Nate missed the children's noisy laughter. Who would have thought it?

Their wives had taken themselves off to the living room with two bottles of wine. "I can hear them giggling," Nate said.

"They're probably laughing at how they conned us into cooking for them. What happened to the badass men we used to be?" Alex cheerfully said as he walked by with plates in his hands.

Court snorted. "Speak for yourself, baby brother. I'm still badass."

By the time they had dinner on the table—roasted pork loin with a raspberry sauce, scalloped potatoes, asparagus, and crusty French bread—the girls, with the exception of Kinsey and only because she was pregnant, were a little tipsy. And a lot funny.

"Did I ever tell you about the time Alex kidnapped me?" Madison asked Kinsey.

"No. This I have to hear."

"Yeah, he stole me right out of my bedroom." She glared at Lauren. "With the help of my roommate."

Lauren smirked. "Didn't hear you protesting any."

"That's beside the point. I'm your best friend. You're supposed to be on my side."

Alex put his mouth next to Madison's ear. "I seem to remember you getting naughty with your abductor," he stage-whispered, making Madison blush.

"That's also beside the point." Then she snickered.

"Come to think of it, Court kidnapped me." Lauren glanced at Kinsey. "I was trying to run away, but the sneaky man caught me and brought me back."

Taylor frowned at Nate. "I'm feeling left out. How come you never kidnapped me?"

"Want me to?"

Her eyes lit up. "Hell, yeah."

"When you least expect it, Tiger." He smiled at her when she put her hand on his leg and squeezed.

Nate ate his dinner—which was surprisingly delicious— listening to his family talk and laugh. A contentment like he'd never before felt settled over him. *I hope you're looking down on us right now, Mama, so you can see how happy your daughter and sons are.*

Dessert was a pinwheel of assorted fancy cheesecakes that a chef friend of Rand's had made for them. Before they dug in, Nate stood and held up his glass of wine.

"A toast. To Taylor, Lauren, and Madison, who tamed three wild boys and taught us how to love." He turned his gaze on his sister. "Kinsey, I know Court and Alex will agree with me on this. If we could choose a sister, she would be you. We're just sorry that it took us so long to find you."

"Amen to that," Court said as Alex nodded.

Nate looked at Rand. "I know we gave you a hard time, but we'd do it—"

"All over again," Rand said without bitterness in his voice.

"Damn straight. We've never had a sister to protect before, and maybe we went a little overboard—"

Kinsey snorted. "A little?"

"Point taken." Nate smiled at her. "But we had to make sure he was good enough for you."

She smiled back at him. "I'll never admit this again, but it was nice having big brothers who thought it was their job to take care of me."

"But just don't do it again?" Alex teased.

"Exactly." Then tears filled her eyes. "I wish Mom were here. She'd be so happy to see us all together."

Nate blinked away his own tears, not missing that his brothers were doing the same. "I think she knows," he softly said. He lifted his glass again. "Merry Christmas."

WHAT'S NEXT FOR SANDRA?

I HAVE A NEW SERIES COMING out that I'm excited about. The first book, *Just Jenny*, in the Blue Ridge Valley series will be out June 26th, so only a few weeks to wait!

SERIES BLURB

The small mountain town of Blue Ridge Valley, located between Asheville, North Carolina, and the Tennessee state line, is the home of three best friends, Jenny Nance, Autumn Archer, and Savannah Graham. Each woman believes she has her life perfectly planned out, but there is a saying in the mountains... *If everything is coming your way, you're in the wrong lane.*

Jenny, Autumn, and Savannah are about to find out how true that is. Surrounded by quirky mountain people who are as nosy as they are loyal, the women will embark on individual journeys, discovering love where they least expect it. Since the people of Blue Ridge Valley cherish a happy ending, they see nothing wrong with lending a helping hand to ensure their hometown girls find their happily ever afters. If that means locking the couple in a basement until they come to their senses or conniving to strand them in a cabin during a snowstorm, they figure all's fair in the name of love.

JUST JENNY BLURB

In *Just Jenny*, Jenny Nance has a plan—save enough money to tour the world. The desire to traipse the globe is a dream she once shared with her twin sister. Jenny made a deathbed promise to her sister that she would go to all the places they had fantasized about visiting together. Nothing will entice her to break her vow to Natalie, not even the sexy new Blue Ridge Valley police chief . . . No matter how attracted she is to him.

Dylan Conrad left the Chicago Police Department to accept the position as chief of police in Blue Ridge Valley. Burned out and haunted by a tragedy of his own, he needs to get away from the memories tormenting him. He's hoping to find peace in the small mountain town, but the quirky residents, an infamous moonshiner, an errant prized bull, and a feisty redhead by the name of Jenny weren't quite what he had in mind.

ACKNOWLEDGMENTS

FROM THE TIME MY FIRST book was published in 2013, I've been on an amazing journey. One of my biggest blessings is the friends I've made around the world. I wish I could name you all, but I'd feel terrible if I missed one of you. But you know who you are, and I'm sending my love to you across the miles.

To all the readers, bloggers, and book reviewers, you guys rock. Thank you for reading my books, for the e-mails telling me how much you love a hero or heroine, a book, or the series, and most of all, thank you for leaving a review. You have my heartfelt gratitude.

This acknowledgment wouldn't be complete without telling you how awesome my reader group, Sandra's Book Salon, is! I think I have the most fun reader group in existence. Thank you for your support and the laughs. I love you all. I'm not going to thank you for your impatience on waiting for my next book, and I'll never admit how much I love that you want it in your greedy hands like RIGHT NOW!

The publishing world changes every day, so much so it's sometimes hard to keep up with. On the business side, people come and go. One constant in this writing life is my critique partner, Jenny Holiday. We've been together since before either one of us was published, and our career paths have been remarkably similar. We've whined to each other, ranted together about things, critiqued everything we've each written, but best of all we've been blessed to be able to celebrate some awesome successes together. Thank you, Jenny, for being my friend and always having time for me.

To my beta readers, you ladies are the best! Brandy, Clarissa, Doni, Heather, Jackie, and Jill, thank you for loving this author's books. I've been lucky to get to personally meet three of you, and someday I hope to meet the rest of you.

To Miranda Liasson and A.E. Jones, two fantastic authors, thank you for being a friend and for the fun e-mails, and for the sometimes early reads. I value your comments and suggestions.

Ah, editors… those are the people an author has a love/hate relationship with. What? How can you say I should delete this or that scene? That's my darling and you want me to kill it? But you know what, they are almost always right. To Melody Guy, my developmental editor, my stories wouldn't be half as good without your (usually) gentle hand. This book makes our ninth one together, and I only hope that we have a long future together.

To Ella Sheridan, my copy editor and proofreader, thank you for making me look smarter than I am. You just need to give up on making me grasp the proper uses of commas, though. You'll be a lot happier for it. Seriously, though, thank you for being an awesome copy editor.

Last and far from least, thank you, family. Jim, Jeff, and DeAnna, you are my world!

ABOUT SANDRA...

BESTSELLING, AWARD-WINNING AUTHOR SANDRA OWENS lives in the beautiful Blue Ridge Mountains of North Carolina. Her family and friends often question her sanity but have ceased being surprised by what she might get up to next. She's jumped out of a plane, flown in an aerobatic plane while the pilot performed death-defying stunts, gotten into laser gun fights in Air Combat, and ridden a Harley motorcycle for years. She regrets nothing.

Sandra is a Romance Writers of America Honor Roll member and a 2013 Golden Heart Finalist for her contemporary romance *Crazy for Her*. In addition to her contemporary romantic suspense novels, she writes Regency stories.

Sign up to Sandra's newsletter to get the latest news, cover reveals, and other fun stuff:
https://bit.ly/2FVUPKS
Join Sandra's Facebook Reader Group:
https://bit.ly/2K5gIcM
Follow Sandra on Bookbub:
www.bookbub.com/authors/sandra-owens

CONNECT WITH SANDRA:
Facebook: *https://bit.ly/2ruKKPl*
Twitter: *https://twitter.com/SandyOwens1*
Goodreads: *https://bit.ly/1LihK43*

Follow Sandra on her Amazon author page:
https://amzn.to/2I4uu2Y

Made in the USA
Coppell, TX
03 June 2021